Author photo by Nicholas Herrmann

HOW WE ARE TRANSLATED

Jessica Gaitán Johannesson grew up between
Sweden, Colombia, and Ecuador. She's a
bookseller and an activist working for climate
justice and lives in Edinburgh. *How We Are
Translated* is her first novel.

JESSICA GAITÁN JOHANNESSON

HOW WE ARE
TRANSLATED

SCRIBE
Melbourne • London

Scribe Publications
2 John St, Clerkenwell, London, WC1N 2ES, United Kingdom
18–20 Edward St, Brunswick, Victoria 3056, Australia
3754 Pleasant Ave, Suite 100, Minneapolis, Minnesota 55409, USA

Published by Scribe in 2021

Front cover images: Thistle by Rowena Naylor, Viking ship by suteishi, Mouse
by Maksim-Manekin
Spine image by Bonninstudio

Typeset in Bembo by the publishers

Printed and bound in the UK by CPI Group (UK) Ltd, Croydon CR0 4YY

Scribe Publications is committed to the sustainable use of natural resources and
the use of paper products made responsibly from those resources.

978 1 950354 82 5 (US edition)
978 1 913348 06 9 (UK edition)
978 1 925849 95 0 (Australian edition)
978 1 925938 78 4 (ebook)

Catalogue records for this book are available from the National Library of
Australia and the British Library.

scribepublications.com
scribepublications.co.uk
scribepublications.com.au

For my mother, Olga Johannesson,
porque esta es la hora y el mejor momento.

Of this enormous Babel of a place I can give you
no account in writing.

Thomas Carlyle about London, 1824

Dime con quién andas
y te diré quién eres.

Tell me who you hang out with
and I'll tell you who you are.

Spanish language proverb

A furore Normannorum,
libera nos Domine.

From the fury of the Northmen,
deliver us O Lord.

Apocryphal phrase

OUT HERE

I can't talk to you right now. You've stopped listening, and we're supposed to go to sleep like it's any other night. We're alive and above water, unlike the inhabitants of your specimen jars. Their eyes are particularly beady tonight. The flat is quiet except for the occasional shrieking fox on the street, a hollering or two from a drunk or tired — *oh so tired* — person. They're normal sounds of a Sunday night, hovering in front of our silence like someone trying to hide a huge balloon from a birthday child. The whole bedroom is dressed up in normal, with the jars on the mantelpiece hovering, too. As long as you're turned toward the wall, I can still tap my knuckle against the back of your head and say:

'Night-knock, Bobe.'

And you always pretend to be asleep already when I do that. It's not announced on the back of your head that this time you've locked yourself in.

Sheet, there was something I needed to ask you. There's only a wrinkle of bedding between us and, just now, only the sound of your soles against the fabric, which is suspicious because it sounds so much like another normal. This is how normal speaks around here, and it's a ficking extraordinary liar. So close to the future, normal is not itself anymore, no matter what it sounds like. Normal is playing dress-up.

3

I take myself out to the lounge and sit on the floor by the bookcase, at eye level with your medical encyclopaedia, which has a smudge on the spine, most likely the only thing that's left in this world of one particular bug. Compared to the specimen jars, the encyclopaedia is easy to stare at for a while. When I look at the jars for longer than a minute, the contents begin to twirl and twist in and out of sight like contrary children being bathed. Fixated, you said, is the technical term. It's a word that pretty much describes you, according to your ma — nailed to a cause, one terrible world-sadness at a time, currently the decline of singing birds and the cuts in care for the elderly. Currently, and then not anymore, because of the future coming along and saying:

Hej du

The foxes are squealing; the drunk people are up and about, too, and the whole other side of the world, until morning. Something other and so unsure underneath my lungs.

Your ma said that she thought your obsession with preserving things came from a crush you had on a biology teacher in high school. I'm told that this teacher had an unfortunate chin even though it wasn't double. 'Ciaran has always had a thing for lab coats,' your ma says. It will upset you that I know this, and this is why I'm mentioning it.

Sometimes I wave to Squirrel McCamp when leaving the bedroom. It feels rude not to when he's always waving back, in spite of himself. You put him in this position. You choreographed him, then left him. When I don't wave this time it's a task left unfinished, a thread of yarn dangling behind me into the dark pool of the bedroom. Squirrel McCamp stands very chilled in there, with his paw gently raised in his jar. *Hiya, Kristin! Hiya K-bit! Hiya, Whoever the Fick You Are Right Now!* You still haven't told me where you found him. I'm a fan of your stories of findings and keepings.

This is all so extremely unnecessary. Your new fixation is a leak the size of my arse when it's open. See? I am also capable of using words you'd never seen me with before.

You said you wanted to 'immerse' yourself in 'my language' to 'prepare'. 'For both our sakes,' you said, which is NOT an answer to why you're JUST NOT HERE ANYMORE. Nurse Roberts-to-be. You think you do everything for other people, but nobody learns a skill that will end up on their CV and potentially strengthen their chances of getting a job with international opportunities for the sake of another person. Nobody learns a language just to be nice, and it pisses me right off that you think that's the case, or that I'm going to believe you think it is. This is your new thing and it's left me queueing.

By the way, Swedish isn't going to help you much if your future is within the NHS. And anyway, didn't you say there was no future?

'Jag är ledsen,' you said.

5

It's possible I've never heard you say 'I am sad' in English. When you are feeling sad you don't say anything, or you talk incessantly about engines and the Paris Agreement. 'I know,' I say. 'It wasn't good enough.' When you need to apologise, you simply say that you're sorry.

It's getting close to two am and you are stewing in there with your specimens. It's a good thing I leave my work at work. If I took to bringing home the Solveig costume, or a sword, this place would soon feel like we weren't living, only selling in it. Nothing would talk to anything else. Looking around the lounge now, time is not visibly passing through it. What's left behind from the day is wrapping itself around furniture and clinging to corners, but it doesn't change, doesn't make a face. The dark can't be exactly the same from one hour to the next, but staring into it halts its progress. It's like watching dough rise. I can't turn my back on it. The future might barge in.

You told me that you printed out and saved our old messages to each other, back in the 'early on', the 'first times', the 'beginning of things', to keep them safe the day the internet crashes. What a blinded end to plan for. The day the internet crashes, it will probably be because of everything else having crashed first just out of sight. They will make it so. It's a shame we don't write emails to each other anymore. I liked re-reading the best things you say.

I'm up for being a grown up with you,

you wrote once.

As if I'd asked you to give ficking pottery a go.

Morning will get here and get inside, even if this was the best kind of night, which it obviously isn't. Tonight has to win at something, such as being full of epiphanies or knife crimes.

Thursday

was when you started it.

On Thursdays we normally watch an episode of *Lost* from your box set, 'drip-feeding' it to ourselves (your words, you're the nurse) the way TV shows used to be consumed back in the day. In a measured way, one episode at a time, never binging. Sometimes I suspect you're not as attached to rituals as I am and then you say something like, 'Let's not be pacified like the rest of these fuck-zombies', and it reminds me of why I live with you and not with any of said fick-zombies. How long can people live together, though, as in live TOGETHER, without speaking the same language?

You met me at the bus stop halfway down Leith Walk and went straight into telling me about Mrs Pullingham's dress. The way you talk about the old people bunches them all together into something very loving, an ecosystem, as if they knew each other and you were all pals, when in fact you spend half of your working day running from one flat to the other to heat up lunches and mount compression socks. I much prefer the illusion of one peach-coloured dining room where they all sit and mildly abuse you. You dispense spoons and inappropriate jokes about deceased musicians they never expect you to know about. You refer to them all as 'Mr' and 'Mrs' which sounds like they're positions in a governing body instead of men and women with bits and, in some cases, lice. In Sweden, titles were thrown out in the sixties, to usher in the welfare state.

We walked at a smooth, familiar tempo, no one hurrying the other along.

'What's Mrs Pullingham's real name?' I said.

'Mrs Pullingham,' you said. 'She's not a spy. She's the one who used to be a stripper, though.'

'The racist one,' I said.

'It's generational, K,' you said. 'By the way, Mr Strachan and I were staring at this cereal box today and he said, "Pal, do you think that man is always waist-high in corn because he's really a flamingo?"'

'She is mildly racist,' I said. 'At least a five out of ten.'

'Because you can't see his legs, like? He's certainly hiding something in that field.'

'She said you must be very grateful because everything is so clean in this country.'

'I fuckin' love Mr Strachan,' you said.

'At least mildly racist,' I repeated. 'What was it she said about you being adopted? That they got you *in time*?'

'Leave her alone. Also, if you keep using your sleeve to wipe your nose, you'll become allergic to cotton.'

'Bullsheet,' I said. 'Didn't she say that *everyone* in Brazil is bloody gorgeous?'

'She knew that tiger worms are endangered. She said I must have a decent stomach to have gutted a squirrel. I need to remember to take a picture to show her.'

You call the animals in the jars the 'bedroom guys', or the 'wee ones'. I call them your specimens. They are artefacts, dead, totally safe and untouchable to change.

You smelt a bit of disinfectant and a lot of sweat. Your elbows were getting dry again. I heard your mum tell you a few weeks ago that you should get that checked out because if you're going to become a nurse, you can't be grossing patients out with suspected skin conditions. You both thought I was on the phone, dealing with a cow-related issue. In fact, the vet had already hung up on me by that point. I was giving your mum the finger through the bedroom wall: your skin is not a condition.

'I don't like it when people assume that you're not Scottish,' I said now.

You looked like you wanted to laugh and I was a road bump.

'You're not my xenophobe guardian, K-bot,' you said. 'I've got it.'

Is it attractive when you sound like someone arriving at a crime scene? We were almost home now. I was urgently trying to remember what was so important about tiger worms, why we should be particularly worried about them. Because you know more about great dangers, I rely on you to prioritise them for me.

'Actually,' you said, 'that's an arsey thing to say. Just maybe lay off with the guardianship when I'm trying to tell you about my day? And when I'd like to hear about yours? How are Lady Gaga's udders?'

When I first met you, I asked where you were from. The second after I asked, I became one of THEM and then I stayed there for a long time, just couldn't rewind. You took a moment to really scoop up it up, from the earth or something, and said very slowly:

'Whit are ye on aboot?'

Sometimes it's like I'm still climbing my way back up from the pit of THEM. I could have just meant 'Where in Scotland are you from?' but obviously I didn't.

'Sorry,' I said. 'You were saying that you stole a ninety-year-old's dress.'

'What happened was I put it in the wash for her and some of the glittery stuff came off. I reckon I can sew it back on. It was the dress in which she met Jimmy Savile.'

'Charming.'

'She loves that thing. She calls it one of her "most treasured possessions". Fuckin' hell, K. Can I keep doing this until I'm fully baked?'

'You're always taking care of things, Bobe. You're the ultra-nurse.'

'Do I want to be a nurse though?' you said. 'Is that going to be the thing?'

'You do,' I said. 'You want to be a nurse so badly.'

I know things for sure about you that I'm only guessing at with

11

anyone else. When I question this, which is more often than is useful, I wonder if it's because I didn't grow up here, and you are part of where I didn't grow up. You are not the gelatinous stillness which tackles people sideways when they return home, leaving them

     hudlös   skinless

one of my favourite Swedish words, incidentally. It's used to mean exposed, vulnerable, but doesn't that give way too much credit to skin? As if skin is armour and not the first thing to go.

I'm not very good with places, whereas you love them and they always seem to take to you. I don't mean the people, necessarily, but everything around them. You looked at my hands; really, you were looking at a Minstrels bag on the ground before you picked it up and threw it in the nearest bin, saying 'fuck's sake'. Every piece of rubbish deserves at least one 'fuck's sake'. I wondered how hungry you were, compared to how hungry I was, and then I began to wonder about lots of people's hunger, including Mrs Pullingham's. You sniffed at your own fingers to check something, then you stopped for a second and coughed even though you didn't have a cold. Where did you come from, to end up next to me, me knowing when you have colds?

    'So how was *your* day?' you said. 'How are you feeling, and so on and so forth?'

    'Ah blah,' I said.

    '*Ah blah* as in terrible or *ah blah* nothing special?'

    You stopped again. I kept walking.

    'Björn Skifs is getting this rash on her right ear. Someone asked me if the blood eagle really existed for the third time in a week. They were carrying a notepad.'

'You can always ignore them,' you said and started walking again, a few steps behind me.

'I just gave him some porridge. Do you think maybe I have a duty to report it if someone wants a detailed explanation of blood eagles?'

'Probably not,' you said. 'What do I know?'

Okay then.

'What's up with you?' I said.

'I asked you how you were feeling.'

'I'm fine,' I said, and grabbed the receipts you were fiddling with. I put them all in my own pocket.

'That's great,' you said.

'Thank you,' I said.

'K,' you said.

'Yes, Bobe.'

'Have you or have you not made an appointment yet?'

A squirrel appeared behind two rubbish bins, not the same kind as McCamp, a real chunky with a fantastic waist. Half its body wasn't catching up fast enough. There might have been a problem in its life.

If I've done the counting right, it's been ten weeks and two days since the start of Project. If I'd found out about it six months ago, it would have been more difficult to pin down the starting date. We were fucking a lot more around that time. About three years ago I decided that I can use the word 'fucking' as a verb, but not as an insult. This is because taking the word into one's mouth and applying it to someone or something other changes them, changes it. Fucking bus driver. Fucking rain. Whereas fucking as an activity happens both ways in a best-case scenario. It does with us. After five years in the UK, I'm not local enough to say 'fucking Tories' but I can say I fucked you.

'Can we agree on something?' I said.

    'You have a gap between your front teeth because of a football.'

    'Ah but I do!'

    'You only know how to draw pigs.'

    'And the satanist symbol.'

    'What do you want?' you said.

    'We'll stay as usual until Wednesday.'

    I ignored the third 'fuck's sake' in five minutes and grabbed your hand.

    'What does that even mean, "as usual"?'

    I haven't grabbed your hand since.

    'Normal. Doing all the things we normally do.'

    'Going to the doctor is normal under these circumstances. That is what people do so they know what to do next. Bringing a hip flask of Lagavulin to work under these circumstances is not normal.'

    'Wednesday,' I said. 'I'll make an appointment on Wednesday.'

    'Kristeeeeen,' you said and did a little shiver.

We were watching a Swedish film the other day, and you heard someone say Kristin in Swedish. The way you've been throwing it in every now and then is like when a child has learnt a word such as 'extraordinary' or 'balls' and is giving it their absolute all.

'What if something happens before Wednesday?' you said. 'Do we just wait?'

'You aren't supposed to do anything just now except look after old people.'

'The old people think you should go see a doctor, too.'

'You did ficking not!'

'Of course, I didn't. You promise, it will be Wednesday?'

'I don't know what it feels like yet,' I said.

Your hand fell away from mine and into a coma. When I tire you out, I wish there was a button to make everyone else take care of you instead.

While you were inside the Co-op, I opened your rucksack to look at the Jimmy Savile dress. It was plastering the bottom of the bag like the starry sky which was missing up there, above Great Junction Street. A visible evening would have helped frame things. You were talking the other day about how we can't trust the seasons, either. Only night and day will stay the same, unless the whole planet is thrown out of orbit. This isn't a consolation. The end of July has always been my least favourite time of year anyway, because it sits in the throat of summer and refuses to be swallowed. When I was about six or seven, pastel and lukewarm nights like these made me queasy. I took it personally that people were still washing cars at ten pm, if I was supposed to be sleeping. Either I or the light were obviously doing something illegal. It's not as bad here. Because I'm twenty-four, and not seven, and because it's here and not Umeå, not quite as far up north.

We came home, very normally. We rattled keys, normally. You tried to memorise the exact order of Mr Strachan's medications from six am to ten pm just in case someday you find yourself without access to his records. The neighbour had left their kids' artwork, a dislodged mannequin-arm with the words 'WOULD YOU LIKE A HAND?' painted on it, in the hallway. We made a pizza without tomato base because you'd forgotten to buy the tomatoes. You seemed like you were waiting for someone to come and visit. You act like it's always the landlord or your mother about to arrive when we have people over, and you're to be found standing in shit. Once, you even started dusting me.

'What is it?' I said. 'You've clocked off now. The day says bye.'

You gnawed on a pizza crust but didn't finish it.

'What? Do you feel ill or are you about to burp?'

Still staring at the bit of crust, you looked up at me, smiled like you'd been plugged into a power supply, and said:

'Jag harr bestimt jag will lerymay svenska.'

'Pardon?'

'Leara, lara?' you said.

'What?'

'Lara! Is that right?'

'Lära?' I said. 'Learn.'

'Yes!' you yelled into my ear.

'Learn what? Do you need a drink?' I said, giving you a cushion instead.

16

You tried again, very slowly this time:

'Jag har bestämt att jag   'I have decided that I want to
vill lära mig svenska.'   learn Swedish.'

It took three more repetitions and five different facial exercises for the words to uncurl themselves into something almost like Swedish.

'How about that?' you said.

The odd angles made your voice unfit for the best hovel in the world, ours. It reminded me of waking up in the middle of a summer night back in Umeå and spotting my mum washing the car outside my bedroom window, sipping on a Carlsberg, and listening to the songs everyone else hated.

'How about that?' you said.

'You sound like a farmer,' I said.

Four years in September, Bobe. I was a bit tired of being me already. The first time we met up you told me you were thinking of becoming a nurse and I remember thinking: this boy will look cold in blue, and he will lose himself. You'd just made us late walking a stranger to the station, while also really needing to wee. You aren't always nice, but you are the kindest. Maybe everyone who cares for a living has a secret corner of selfishness, a propensity for hoarding, or an unnecessary number of massage balls. No one seems to know what any of it is for until it comes down to it. It turns out you have been collecting dictionaries.

Two years ago, we came to look at the best hovel — a lounge with a kitchenette in the corner, this almost fluorescent bathtub with no room left for undressing, and one bed-sized bedroom. Your ma insisted on bringing her own measuring tapes, plural. You scavenged for flaws, in spite of your current shared situation with the kickboxer guy and the weed in the meat drawer. Your ma wanted to fill the cupboard to get us started. You said we were fine.

'I have made a list and it's full of protein,' you said.

'Excuse me?' I said again.

'Jag will lera maj swinska,' you said, which was close enough.

'But,' I said, 'we're having a pint with Jenny in about exactly twenty minutes.'

'Ja,' you said.

'Mycket snart.'   'Very soon.'

'Ah, okay,' I said. 'At least we agree that twenty minutes is soon?'

You went to bite your fingernails over the bathroom sink. I could hear the pffft and click of the halfmoons being spat out and hitting the ceramic.

'How did you learn all of that?'

'Duolingo, K-bot. It's brilliant. You translate the internet. And a course pack Mr Strachan's son recommended. He's just spent a semester in Kristianstad! What's Kristianstad like, by the way, is it provincial?'

You even sort of knew how to pronounce Kristianstad.

'Why don't I know that you know all of this?' I said.

Now you were brushing your teeth. You poked your head out, foam dripping, and said: 'It was meant to be a surprise!'

I went to the kitchen cupboard, reached all the way in, and grabbed two bags of Swedish liquorice which I'd asked my parents to send for you in case of a rubbish day. The consume-by date was in four months' time.

'I love surprises,' I said and placed them at your feet.

'Sometimes,' you said. 'When you make an effort.'

It shouldn't be acceptable, having a body and not knowing when something began in it.

överraskning	surprise
över	over
raska	trod
överraskning	to trod over something

Such as the next minute, such as the way forward.

It was a good pint. But the people working there don't really know how to pour. Jenny became drunk and a fan of people's inner ears. I counted the times you asked me what this or that is called in Swedish. Three wasn't so bad, at least not spread out over a few hours, and after that I was too tipsy not to laugh at it. When we came home you threw yourself horizontally across the bed with your head dangling over the edge, to increase the blood flow to the scalp, a method recommended by someone called Dr Hubert.

'You're not going bald,' I said.

'There's no way of knowing, K-gram. My mum is well on her way and it's rare in women, especially of her complexion.'

'Bobe, you're not related.'

'That, also, was a joke,' you said.

You began to energetically massage your skull, stopping and looking for residue on your fingertips.

19

'Why now?' I said.

'Because it can start in your mid-twenties if you're not careful.'

'No, the Swedish, Bobe.'

'Ah!' you said. 'Well.'

You sat up and put your hands on my knees.

'I just feel bad.'

'That's not news,' I said.

'That I've not made an effort before. We've been together for four years.'

'Four is it?'

'Three years, ten months, and seventeen days, and I haven't even tried to learn Swedish.'

'You climbed the Cairngorms, though,' I said.

You also saved at least three wee puffins on Shetland, but if I'd mentioned that you'd start thinking about all the ones you didn't save.

'Wee' is the kind of word I can say even though it's not my place, really, to be saying it. It's the kind of slang people who are not from Scotland adopt to pay tribute, or to show solidarity, depending on where they stand on the independence question.

Later, just as I was falling asleep, you turned on your back out of the darkness and blurted out: 'Things!'

I ignored that.

'The way things are now,' you said.

The neighbour's microwave hollered. The jars kept it to

20

themselves.

'No,' I said. 'Please not now.'

'Okay, well there's nothing wrong with me learning Swedish anyway, just in case. People learn Swedish all the time.'

'I don't like Swedish very much. I don't see why you would want to learn it to be honest.'

You didn't answer and we had some time to wade through that one.

'You know I've never actually chosen to learn a language,' you said. 'They just picked me up over there and plonked me down here.'

I clapped my hands together in the space above our heads and almost killed the fly which had been roaming for ten minutes.

'Don't ever say that to your mother,' I said.

'I'll do it,' you said. 'You know you'll be kept awake by that thing.'

'Besides, neither have I. People don't choose to learn English. It's like smog.'

Fifteen minutes after that you turned the lamp on again, sat up, and reached for your phone.

'Smör,' you hissed into it. 'Smöööööör!'

'Have I ever told you that I'd chosen to become a celibate when I met you?' I said.

'You were twenty years old,' you said. 'Hey, do you want to use my bus pass this week? As I'm off?'

'Is this what you'll be doing, shouting "butter" into your phone? I thought you were taking the week for course stuff.'

Your night voice is artificial. It comes out squeaky clean,

even the second before you fall asleep.

'I've worked it all out,' you said. 'It'll be tremendous.'

You looked at me with one eye. How the fick do you do that?

'I wonder if someone's ever preserved a flamingo in formaldehyde,' you said.

I do like going out, having pints, and I like other people, but since I met you, the end of the night is the best, when we're done but — wow — not yet, somehow, done with each other.

How about if I said what all the people say, as they tumble about, distracted or horny? The thing they say to their grand-aunts, their best pals, and the people they can't help but admire? I LOVE you, oh I love you so much. Well. That's what it feels like, hearing you try to speak Swedish.

It's not necessary to go back to such basics. It's more like us to say what we really mean: you're the most competent at making me laugh. You look almost pretty in that dust bin. I'm sure you're my best friend by now. You have spinach between your teeth. You're like me.

If I were to be pregnant now: nothing would be like us anymore.

Three am. Sleep would be good. Solveig would never fall asleep on the job, making the dry, nutritious bread. She's too focused on the task at hand — that task, in the tenth century AD, being survival. My foot feels like it's being nibbled by small iron ants. I just thought of Mrs Pullingham's dress, which you were going to fix. It's still in your rucksack, three days later. For as long as I've known you, you've been

livrädd   life scared

of being selfish without noticing. Mrs Pullingham's dress proves a point. Where to put it?

It's a shame that you don't snore. At least that would be something coming out of your face which you couldn't make dictatorial decisions about. The light from the lounge windows arranges the shadows on the opposite wall into a great still life. A cushion is transformed into a Pac-Man, the two picture frames become simple yet elegant second homes for rich people, and a potted plant grows rabbit ears and a fat cigar. The odd passing car transmits coded signals. I could describe the entire room through its shadows. Have you ever seen the flat do this? What is the worst thing that could be going on within a five-mile radius, right now? If the worst things happened right now, where would we go?

Literal translations: I've been collecting them for a while, and it's got worse since finding out about Project. They've been cluttering up every single bus-stop ad. Something has pushed English to one side and is digging a ditch. Compound words are especially attention-seeking.

If I were a pregnant person now, it would be a

beslut   decision
be   ask
slut   ending
beslut   to ask for a (certain?) ending

23

Friday

In the morning, nothing seemed much amiss

    a miss   en miss

    one miss   en fröken

    a mistress

    There is no reason I should stop this.

You were playing air guitar whilst waiting for the mocha pot to brew. The way one of your feet was half out of its stolen (from Ernest, your mother's last ex) slipper looked nicely typical.

'That thing is going to spew and very soon,' I said, and sat down to pick the raisins out of my muesli, not wanting to remember how I'd dreamt of fontanelles.

'It's my friend!' you shouted and went across the room to the pot.

I wanted to hug you, but I could tell, by the way you were pouring and creating squares around yourself, that you were in a non-touchy mood. You take a long time exhaling.

'If you could be amazing at playing air anything, what would it be?' you said.

'Air ice hockey,' I said. 'Without the puck or the stick. Maybe without the ice, even.'

24

You closed your eyes and took some time to build that particular nonsense. You always close your eyes when you're considering something carefully, and that's when people see the wee scar on your eyelid. I can ask you to show it to me any time. Now that is radicalism.

'It looks like shite contemporary dance,' you asserted.

'I can't see it,' I said.

'Ooooh, K-face,' you said. 'You don't want to play?'

'That's not what I meant,' I said.

I was almost late for work because I couldn't find my hair pins on the mantelpiece. I had to move Squirrel McCamp and Newtongrange slightly to the left. Behind curved glass everything looks like the thing you're looking for. The hair pins, it turned out, were hidden by the Thumb, which is in the smallest of the jars. I thought it was plastic for about a week. By the time I shook hands with your ma I'd already discovered that you very rarely exaggerate.

'Do you even remember a time before the puffins were in danger?' you said.

'I didn't know what puffins were until five years ago,' I said.

Arriving at the Castle, I went into my Translation Room, came out again, and did the milking. A bit like the word 'lovely' in English, you have to glance sideways at 'Translation Room' for a while before you get the way we use it around here. When we talk about a Translation Room, it's a temporal noun ('During Translation Room the other week I heard an illegal drone fly by

25

my window') as well as a spatial noun ('Inside my Translation Room there is a TV screen from the year 1988'). I've even heard Joanne Tarbuck use it as a verb: 'Time to Translation-Room, pet!' She's worked here for over a decade. It makes me think of Swedish people and the way we treat the word 'fika'.

att fika	to fika: to have a coffee/tea with or without something sweet on the side
en fika	a fika: a tea/coffee, with or without something sweet on the side

And in some parts of Sweden, the fika is just the sandwich.

We're required to spend twenty minutes in our Translation Room before every shift, before we start getting paid. This is how we switch over to our native languages and leave our English-speaking everydays tidily outside. In one of the sci-fi novels you read last year (during the months when you decided that the answers were in sci-fi novels) they would call it an airlock, or a portal, if broom closets made for good portals. People's Translation Rooms are dotted around the Castle (offices, old stables, in one case a toilet cubicle) and used for the purpose of changing into the Peoples we belong to. This is how we're always newly arrived, always immigrants, and don't know much about anything. My Translation Room is a tiny chamber at the top of the Royal Palace clock tower. Before the National Museum of Immigration took over the Castle, it wasn't being used at all. They had to put in a proper window.

'At a considerable cost,' Joanne Tarbuck says.

'About twice as considerable as my salary,' Joanne Tarbuck adds.

I found a tear in my Solveig shift but didn't hand it in to maintenance. They'll only give me another and chuck the old one in landfill. They worry about the costumes ending up in a Fringe production if they're given to charity shops. As a result, I walked with my back against the walls of buildings most of the afternoon. Once, a visitor filed a complaint because they'd had their trousers stained with soot when walking past the Lithuanians. It was explained to the visitor in question that the Lithuanians came to Scotland as coal miners. They couldn't help that, of course, but they would be more careful with not spreading their soot to people who had nothing to do with it. The visitor was given free-entry vouchers.

There's no need to spend time in your Translation Room at the end of the day. How we speak once the day is over is of little to no consequence with regards to visitor satisfaction. When my shift had technically finished, Joanne Tarbuck caught up with me in the Royal Palace staircase and asked me if the Norse had submitted a bid for leading the Summer Parade on Monday. When I said no, she looked disappointed. She asked me to stay behind and help Barbara in the ticket office swap the old edition of the welcome brochure for a new version. There's been talk of a new brochure for months, but the only change, it turns out, is that the word 'Castle' doesn't feature anywhere in the text anymore. The National Museum of Immigration wants to encourage the public to call it by its official name, or at least to use the acronym.

Every time I hear people, you in particular, still referring to the place where I work as the Castle, it makes me feel like someone's won a little battle. What you see is, in essence, still a Castle. You are not lying.

Barbara's family came here from Syria. I've never dared ask her how all that happened and now it's way too late.

'I thought they would have done something new,' she said, flicking through the brochure.

She spat on the middle spread, with the pictures of the Summer Parade on it, then she smoothed the brochure shut and filed it with the others in the stand. There is no Syrian exhibition at the National Museum of Immigration, nor is there one, as far as I know, in the pipeline. Three Pakistani teenagers working in the restaurant petitioned for the Pakistani community to be represented, but the request has been denied due to the need for maintenance of existing exhibitions. East Bu, the Norse exhibition, has an entire page to itself.

'So,' Barbara said, 'you will be putting on helmets Monday, yes?'

The Summer Parade happens every year the week before the festivals kick off, to remind people that it's worth paying £20 to come and see us, even with hundreds of free shows available. There's even a show about the Norse gods this year. I'm told that it's narrated by the ravens. Every year, each People suggests a very important contribution its culture made to Scotland. The best suggestion gets to lead the Parade. Nobody at East Bu bothers with it, except for Ingrid who takes part out

28

of principle. Her submissions always include three appendices with references to digging sites. Once, we found a whole wad of these in the recycling bin where we get paper for the funeral pyres.

'We've never worn helmets,' I said to Barbara. 'Not even once.'

'The Irish will win anyway,' she said. 'That is okay.'

I agreed that the Irish are okay. I was about to say that I was sorry about the brochures, but Barbara kept side-glancing at me whilst folding up the empty cardboard boxes. She was right. People say 'I'm sorry' all the time when it can mean both 'I'm sorry I hurt you' and 'I'm sorry someone else did something I have nothing to do with'. It's like the English language gave up on trying to find a word for sympathy which wasn't also the word for guilt.

This is what you looked like when I came home: wrinkled and bored, ostensibly with the shortbread-colour of our floor. There were three newspapers spread out on it and two books open on the lounge table. One of them already with two mug-prints of instant coffee.

'I hope those are from the library,' I said.

'Gokwall!' you said, which should have been:

'God kväll!'   'Good evening!'

You threw your arms up and got up off the floor.

'God kväll på dig själv,'   'Good evening yourself,'

I said, because I still felt bad about Barbara. I told you about the brochure, how they hadn't included any new Peoples.

29

'What if they're building a kingdom and I don't like it?' I said.
You

spärrade   pried/blocked your eyes open,

                                            trying to catch something.

'Mycket synd,'   'Much shame,'

you nodded.

'That's really good,' I said.

'But I sound like a very white girl from the fifties, right?'
you said. 'Improvement is everything.'

You closed all the books and put them to one side neatly in a
pile next to the feathers from Shetland. One of them was *Asterix
& Obelix* in Swedish. I had one as a child and it used to worry
me because my dad had terrible back problems. That ominous,
phallic rock. I asked you how your first day off had been.

'Great,' you said. 'That's bad, though. About the new
Peoples.'

'Well they're not new,' I said. 'That's what's sheet about it.'

'Maybe I should come see you at work,' you said. 'Hang out
with the Vikings. That would help.'

'It's Norse people,' I said. 'They only hang out with
themselves.'

There are immigrants and then there are immigrants. Some
are brutal and some are ancient. Solveig is both ancient and brutal
and that's why I don't particularly want you hanging out with her.

Crumbs from all your new knowledge were spread across the lounge,
and in the bedroom. I found pages from websites about how to get
by at Systembolaget, at a hotel, in a synagogue, and explaining about

30

one's taxes. The last one you had folded into a little boat and set sailing in the sink. There were hand-written lists of Swedish verbs and pronouns as well as several maps of Stockholm in the fifties, with made-up names of residents: Gunnar the Ornithologist lives here. At some point, you'd purchased a blackboard which was now filled with small ghoulish faces illustrating the way the mouth forms the å, the ä, and the ö. I wanted to tell them to simply close their mouths and everything would be much easier.

'Have you had twice as many hours as I have today?'

'In Swedish you say half two when we say half three,' you said.

I found your phone next to the loo. Sometimes I take your phone with me in there to binge on useless news: which celebrity has a sister you didn't know about but who looks SO like them, chickens adopted by cats who were later eaten by a rare eagle in Surrey. I like to think about what it does to your search history, knowing that you do care a bit about that kind of thing. This time you'd been browsing an article about immersion language courses. The guy who wrote it had done a three-year Arabic degree and graduated without being able to hold a conversation that wasn't about football or the stock exchange. He then went on a two-month immersion course, during which he wasn't allowed to speak any English whatsoever, not even to apologise when he stepped on someone's toe. He swore by the efficiency of the method. I'd almost read the whole thing by the time you knocked.

'You don't have time to take two months off!' I shouted.

'It's too hot to have baths, K-bits. Also, the *water*!'

31

You made an omelette and I discovered that at some point in the past month eggs have become evil. You hid mine in a wholemeal bap and gave it to me with a 'Varsågod', but that only made it worse.

Watching me try to swallow you said: 'Do you think it's because of the —'

'Blip.' I said.

'Projects require a plan,' you said. 'We need a division of labour.'

'Blip it,' I said.

'Are you going to want an apple?'

'Blip. Ficking eggshell!' I said.

I went to make sure it ended up in the sink. My tonsils tasted like fish.

After you opened the windows, you started talking about a book you'd been reading. It claimed that, in reality, we actually don't think in one specific language. If we did, nobody would be able to say things like 'that's not what I meant'. There would be no 'what I meant' to compare with.

'Do you remember in the beginning-times?' you said. 'When you woke up and told me in detail about murders in Swedish films? I asked you stuff, too, when you were asleep, and you always answered in Swedish. I asked you what we should name the First Mouse and you talked for like half a minute.'

'I don't do that anymore, do I? Talk about the murders.'

'I miss it a little,' you said. 'You know in Swedish they call it sproke bad.'

32

'Sorry?'

'Sprooooookbad?'

'Oh,' I said,

'Språkbad!'   'Language bath!'

You peeled your lower lip over your gums to try and dislodge something from between your teeth. Everything was so great again. You looked like a frog travelling at high speed.

'Isn't that brilliant?' you said. 'Imagine if you could take a bath and then come out understanding someone else's language.'

'I told you I didn't take a bath. I was looking through your messages. Who's Hector by the way?'

'He lives in Göööööteborg, he drives a taxi and plays D&D.'

You're very excited about starting daily conversation with Hector.

At about nine pm, Denise passed right underneath our window, singing her usual version of 'Poker Face'. I've only spoken to her once and she said, 'Are you with that black lad?' Then she gave me a Sharpie.

You said: 'So, K-meter, this is how it will work.'

You were in your pants, a T-shirt, and socks. Bouncing up to the blackboard, you began to list activities next to times. The next few days were going to begin with two hours of grammar studies, from nine am. Then listening to Sveriges Radio and making notes about what you thought the programme might be about. After lunch it's pronunciation online followed by watching Swedish TV and films until I come home.

'What happens if you want to see someone?' I said.

33

'Then I keep it under one hour,' you said.

'For how long?'

'Until Wednesday,' you said.

That kept me quiet.

Denise was on the second round of 'Poker Face' when she passed the house on her way back. You pressed your cheek against the window and insisted that you could feel the vibrations. I told you my parents were disappointed with me for having given you all the liquorice at once.

'She's on good form tonight,' you said. 'Denise.'

'Where do you think she leaves all her stuff? Doesn't she worry about having it stolen?'

'Eh,' you said. 'At home?'

'What?' I said. 'But she's homeless.'

You looked at me briefly and then out the window again.

'No, she's not. She used to be part of my team at work before she became psychotic. She had a breakdown in Mr Lewis's laundry basket, started singing that song when she was picking up his shirts, and didn't stop.'

Three years ago, I named one of the cows at work Lady Gaga. It was in honour of Denise. I did it to remind myself not to forget the people who aren't right in front of me, because you never seem to.

'I can't concentrate,' I said.

The day I found out, I took five tests in total and spent £100 at Boots. The man asked me if I had a Boots card and I said that, sadly, no, I didn't, but he didn't offer to start one up for me. 'Shame, that,' was all he said. He was imagining all those points, probably. Maybe he thought that, considering what I'd spent the money on, it was bad taste to take advantage, that it would suggest a likelihood of me being back soon for further pregnancy tests, label me some kind of loose cannon. The first test was at home in the morning, before you woke up. Waiting for it to go blue, I chanted:

> med barn
>
> med barn
>
> med barn
>
> med barn

the way I recited someone else's name in my head when the winner of a competition at the end of fifth grade was about to be announced. I was preparing for the unwanted so as to protect myself. Only then, in fact, did I know which outcome was unwanted. I'm not too young for a child and I'm not too old either. We don't have great jobs but we have them. On the surface, yet within sight, everything is pretty okay.

I hate the word PREGNANT, its heavy sponge, ready to flop from a height and hit someone in the head. WITH CHILD is even worse. It makes me think of the yellow traffic signs used on school routes, with one big and one small person. It looks like a T-shirt: 'I'm with stupid!', 'I'm with child!'

> med barn   with child

The second test was at work, just after I got changed into the Solveig clothes, but before I went into my Translation Room. The Solveig clothes are a lot easier to wee in, and to do anything else in

35

which requires weeing. Getting rid of the test proved problematic, as other people use the same Translation Room before and after me. I ended up wrapping it in loo roll and tucking it under the waistband of my pants. The third and fourth tests were both taken at home, but it still wasn't time to say anything, by any means. I have a bad history of telling things too soon. When I was ten, I thought I'd just detected my first period, a rusty miniature Italy in my pants, and ran out to the kitchen to tell my mother, but it turned out I was about to spend two days in bed with a stomach bug. Telling too soon mistakes shit for blood. Five years ago, I wrote my first note to myself in English, about buying Fairy Liquid. It was the day after we had our first conversation. This is it, I thought, from now on, you are an English-speaking person. With this person, you will be an English speaker. And then the next day I wrote something else, and looked at it, and it was, ah fick, the word BÖCKER. What was it about books? Who knows?

I held on till the next morning, wanting to be sure. I didn't want to not only have to take it back, but take it back for both of us. Then I took a fifth test. Then I waited in the space between the couch and the bookshelf for you to come home. You'd been playing video games with your pal Lucas and, you explained, the two of you were currently stuck with a wee man between two giant acorns.

'What do you want to do?' was the first thing you said after I'd divulged.

What you didn't say was:

Adoption is an option. Look at how I turned out!

36

or

Are you sure it's mine?

You most certainly didn't say:

I have no idea how to keep it safe out there, the way things are going.

'What do you want to do?' you said.

Why didn't you say something no one has ever said before?

If I were to have a kid now, you'd have to learn how to say so many things so very, very quickly. When we talked about this kind of thing before, you said you'd want to build exemplary dens, the kind that kids love enough to want their dinners in. We have talked about kids before, but we don't talk about kids now. Right now, I can't even think of the Swedish word for den.

It's a quarter to four in the morning. I fall asleep for a bit and a square of knitted cushion-terrain etches itself onto my cheek, like maths to the touch. The dark is no different from the dark of an hour ago, and we are edging closer to Monday, from one week to the next, when some minor, some inexplicable things, will be too late to take back. There is a gurgling in the walls, spreading from top to bottom. If something terrible happened to this building, to this street, would it be helpful to be high up? We'd have further to run but we'd also be further away from dangerous and scared people. Unless we're the dangerous and scared people. Denise isn't in so much danger anymore. That's good.

I don't tell you that I also think about this stuff. I'm afraid we will never give anything a stupid name again after that. You'd say that because we live up high, we'd have the chance to get more people on the way down, that the way we escape would matter.

As to the jugular sound, it's probably just gravity not being finished. Your mum is bound to start panicking about that when she comes back from her yoga retreat. I wouldn't think this is when you'd want to be reminded of gravity. I always remember if you've said something to me or if you've written it because of the face that comes along with it. They are both you, but going down different avenues, different passages in me. I have so many emails from you. We loved writing them, because when we got together, we were both terrible at 'on the spot'. You were also spending a lot of time on Shetland, with the puffins. You sent me pictures of puffins. Although you've had time to erase, retract, and smooth out, your old emails still feel more immediate sometimes, than what you say across our table. In one late-night email you told me about going to the swimming pool with your mum when you were four and getting changed with the many confusing women. You looked for people who were boys and who looked at least a little bit like you, at least from far away.

I was looking for someone within my league,

you wrote.

I knew you so very little and you didn't mean what I thought you meant at all.

If we were to have a boy, he would look odd. I wouldn't wish my rat-tail hair on anyone.

Saturday

The schedule begins at nine o'clock sharp, but before that, horrifically, there's the weather across Scandinavia. The report is delivered with gusto, but the theme song reminds me of a dish my dad used to make called 'kallops'.

I said: 'I used to fancy that guy so much, but he used to have a slightly different way about him.'

'You have exactly twenty minutes,' you said, even whilst holding me. 'Then the day begins.'

There was another little list next to the main schedule on the blackboard. It included 'call mother' and 'inject toad'. The latter was brilliant news. You haven't preserved anything new in a few weeks and there isn't enough room in the freezer for my peas next to the animals.

'Those are all the things I need to get done before the day starts,' you said.

A huge cloud came over the west, moving from our island to Scandinavia.

'What's "climate collapse" in Swedish?' you said, and one of your hands twitched.

'Klimatkallops,' I said.

You wrote that down.

'I'm so sorry,' I said. 'That's not right. That's "climate stew".'

When you dropped a glass of water and said 'mother cracking fucker!' it was beautiful. We made out for a while then. I pointed at the shards of glass on the floor.

'Glas,' you said.

I pointed at the contents of your breakfast bowl.

'Gröt!' you said.

'It's kind of like watching an athlete learn to walk,' I said. 'Could you focus just on body parts today and then, when I get home, we'll go to bed to put it into practice?'

'But Kristeeen,' you said and pointed at the blackboard. 'Look at the schedule! If I don't spend time on propositions today, I won't know where your boobs are.'

You do this. It was butterflies for a while. One of them looked like a small person's shrivelled ear. I was trying very hard to get to the place where it becomes sexy to see you so full to the brim. Now. How about now?

There was a text from Mr Batsford, one of the Castle janitors, saying that something seemed off with Lady Gaga, although he obviously didn't call her that. The cows' real names are irrelevant because they don't respond to them. Mr Batsford refers to 'the white' and 'the spotty' one. The spotty one was making that funny sound in her throat again, he wrote, and should he call the vet. Christ, I replied, call the vet. Always call the vet. You'd gone into the bathroom to brush your teeth.

'I have to go now!' I shouted.

'Aaaaand GO!' you said and ran to the table.

'Wow, I didn't know people could run in this flat!'

It was exactly nine am.

'Have you seen your bus pass?' I said. 'I meant to borrow it again today.'

'Ursäkta?'   'Pardon?'

you said.

You waved through the window down at Tall Azif who was leaving for work.

'Bobe, please,' I said. 'Bus pass.'

'Why does she call you that?' your ma said only once.

'Because other people say "babe",' you told her.

'Ah,' she said. 'I thought it was because of Roberts.'

It took you five minutes to look up the words 'jacket' and 'pocket' in the dictionary. By that time, I had missed my bus.

'Look,' you said. 'How do you think Chris Hadfield became an astronaut?'

'What, really, are you on about?'

'Self-discipline.'

'You're against space travel,' I said.

'Harsh,' you said.

Lady Gaga was constipated. The vet fed her olive oil through a bottle and she gulped it down, looking shocked. My eyes teared up when hers were drying up. When there's something wrong with the cows, Mr Batsford calls me first. One of these days someone will remind him that I'm a history graduate who knows sheet about animal welfare. Knowing *these* cows doesn't

41

mean I know about cows. Back in Solveig's time, though, she would have been the person who knew the cows best, their vet and their carer, their herd leader, all thrown into one. Sometimes Björn Skifs looks at me and I remember that we were put in a position where the one thing I can't ever become is their friend.

The vet told me that Joanne Tarbuck has consulted her on the safety of potentially bringing the cows out for the Summer Parade this year.

'Fick,' I said, then checked the surroundings.

There was no one around to take offence.

'Safe for them or for the public?' said the vet. 'Obviously, she's a bell-end.'

I put my hands together in a sign of gratitude. The vet and I communicate through hand signals, complemented by the text messages I send her once I've finished and am back to speaking English at the end of the day. We keep each other up to date that way. The vet thinks this is all nonsense, the speaking only our first languages for authenticity. The first time Björn Skifs had trouble breathing, Joanne Tarbuck was in the room, watching over us.

'Jesus wept,' the vet said. 'I'm here to do my job, not to play charades.'

Since then, she speaks English to me and I'm allowed to understand as long as it's cow-health related. I reply with hand gestures. The cows become agitated. It very rarely feels like we're colleagues.

I sent you two texts throughout the day, one on my lunch break (I'm not supposed to touch my phone between entering and leaving the Castle, but everyone does it) and one on my way home. You replied in terrible, well-meaning Swedish:

'Vi inte har nog ost   'We not have cheese enough
— kan du införskaffa?'   — can you purchase?'

I'm having to turn your translations inside out to understand them.

'Bwahahaha! Breast wart!' you wrote at around four pm, which meant you must have made time for my request after all. I hurried home.

Bröstvårta   Nipple

I must have been very distracted as a child not to have noticed this. We must, as a people, hold nipples in very low regard in Sweden.

There was a Post-it note attached to our front door: 'YTTERDÖRR' it said. That came right off. There's no need to spread this to the whole building. I suspect that the guy upstairs had already seen it, though, because he'd left his juggling gear in the stairwell. It looked too much like a response to be purely accidental. The labelling continued indoors. Discovering the notes, I began to feel very old, very forgetful, not knowing what a kettle is and needing to be reminded of the words for 'utility bill'. You were still smacking names onto various segments of domesticity. FÖNSTER. Tag. BOKHYLLA. Tag. You came over to me where I'd taken refuge by the window. You had just had a shower. You kissed me on the forehead and

43

pressed another Post-it onto it: BÄBIS. I ripped it off.

'People don't call each other "baby" in Sweden unless one of them is an infant,' I said.

'What would you like me to call you?' you said, quite genuinely, I think.

Before dinner, I sat down to read a new article on the Norse graves at Westray, which was hard with you repeating lines in front of your laptop. One of them was about vegetarians not eating bears. Duolingo seems to work on the premise that nonsense is memorable. Sometimes it's the vegetarians not eating the bears, and sometimes the bears are under tables. I asked you when you reckoned the day could end, because it should already have ended.

'Give me ten minutes. I'm so *in* it!' you said.

On the bus home, I'd remembered what it's like to make you look thrilled in a matter of seconds. I sat up and cleared my throat. I kept clearing it until you turned around from the screen.

'Jag blev jagad av en björn en gång,'	'I was chased by a bear once,'

I said.

'Cool!' you said.

'What? You *understood* that?'

'Not exactly, but give me some context and who knows what will happen.'

'I was chased by a bear,' I said.

'Nej! På svenska,	'No! In Swedish,

44

fina groda!'   lovely frog!'

'Right,' I said, 'it's preferable to "bäbis".'

I told you a story about me and my dad mushroom-picking. It happened when my mum was working with a theatre company in Skellefteå. The play was in English; they were staging it for recently arrived refugees. We went for the premiere, and the whole day before the performance, my dad and I hiked in the woods. The look-out towers, used for hunting moose, looked left behind by something much older than last year's hunting season. I found a mulchy, crowded patch of mushrooms on the edge of a swamp,

brandgul trumpetsvamp   fireyellowtrumpetmushroom,

which have brown hats and camouflage really well as leaves until you crouch down and look at the undergrowth sideways, then it's a miniature army. My dad needed to pee and went off to find a secluded spot. He worries a lot about people hearing him pee. I picked the mushrooms into my folded-up jumper. The bear entered with a grunt one hundred and eighty degrees behind my back. I remember thinking not that it was going to kill me, but that it was going to kick me into the swamp, then sit there and point at me, delighted. I set off crawling, then running, then falling and running again. My dad still says that there was no bear. He expressed deep regret about the spilt mushrooms.

'Yes!' you said, 'exactly like that. More of that!'

From the charades and a word here and there, you had understood that there was some picking, of something, from the floor, and that there was a form of beast.

45

After telling it again, this time in English, I showed you where it happened on one of your maps.

'But where did the refugees come from?' you said.

'A war,' I said because you'd caught me off guard.

'You must have known,' you said. 'You would have cared about the refugees.'

We spent the next half hour looking at different bears online.

'Let's do this more often,' you said and made me orange juice from scratch when I became thirsty.

When I came out of the shower, you were already back at it, the day not over after all:

'Avkastningen per	'The quarterly returns
kvartal översteg våra	exceeded our expectations!'
förväntningar!'	

'It probably says something about Swedish,' I said. 'Bears and quarterly returns.'

Some of the domestic labels are already curling at the corners and coming unstuck, dust creeping in and covering the feeble glue under each of them. You're right there, ready to re-do them before they fall off.

Thinking of the word 'hindsight' now. And then it's not now anymore and the hind has been pushed forward. Hindsight is all about holes in the now, a present punctured.

hindsight	baksikt
baking sight	what you can only know once
	the bun is out of the oven

sikt   sieve, full of holes

I should have known this wasn't working.

If we suddenly had to leave this flat, depending on the nature of the suddenly, what would be left behind? How quickly would those traces of us decay and how different would a new home, built up somewhere else, be? Would we never throw our pants on the floor again because it was no longer on that particular floor, and we were different people now, more forward-thinking — aware of having to pick them up again at some point? When I was at uni, there was this guy who wanted to make a career out of knowing everything about the history of interior design, upholstery in the thirties especially, the slightly older layers of wallpaper under some more wallpaper in someone's lounge. Even though he lived in Edinburgh, he had a season ticket to the V&A in London. He mentioned to me, both times we spoke, that they always gave him free coffee in the garden cafe.

I was studying wars. How heavy is the war that leaves not a trace of wallpaper left to study? I still spend a lot of time thinking about our wallpaper, whatever cells from my arse or your hands are stuck to it. You choosing not to speak to me is a sign that you don't think of it as *our* wallpaper in the first place.

I've been reading some of your old emails. They are quite long, especially the ones describing the nature reserve where you were working after dropping out of uni, many different kinds of meadow grass. A paragraph is dedicated to the gloves of

47

people working there, their knuckles, ailments, and how these relate to whatever else was around, the weeds. Like I said, you are good with places. Every email also includes a new way of addressing me, before the time of all the 'Ks':

> I don't recommend shaving your head, mate. You'll be cold, and if you're like me and don't like wearing hats you'll just suffer all the way through winter. You asked me yesterday, before the Scientology guy interrupted us on Nicolson Street, when I shaved my head for the first time. I was twelve. This idiot at school decided to start pulling my hair. The cunt said brown people have thicker scalps so it doesn't hurt so much. I still wonder sometimes, just out of interest, where he got that from. If he has a bell-end uncle. Who it was that made him believe that. I waited three months before I shaved it so he wouldn't think he was the reason. He wasn't going to think he was the reason for anything.

When I was at primary school, the worst thing people could say to someone with dark hair was

    svartskalle   blackskull/blackhead

There were no people with black hair in my school and it had nothing to do with clogged pores.

> My grandmother died last year. She came to Glasgow from Texas when she was nineteen. She had pretty bad

48

dementia and in the last few months of her life she lost
her Scottish accent and began to say 'y'all' and 'darn' to
us when we tried to feed her biscuits. They were her
favourites. I wonder if this means that we could both
lose English one day. How young do you think you
have to be when they give it to you, for a language to
be yours forever? So that it can't be taken away?

Reading back, I wonder who 'they' are. 'They' must have
some pretty spectacular powers. If it's not a 'they' at all but our
own brains, it could mean we were never meant to try to understand so much.

It's four am and practically the night is over. It's almost Monday.
You make a sound in your sleep. Could be your sinuses but also
your bones, a clicking which fick knows if it's serious.

This is still the safest place in the world.

Sunday

Translation Rooms — as for those belonging to others, I'm not sure, but what I do in mine is watch a film for twenty minutes. I also drink tea using tea bags stolen from another Translation Room user and think about how cold it would have been, in Solveig's time, all the brutal ficking time. This morning, there was a swish-swooshing sound right outside the door to my Translation Room.

'Occupied!' I yelled.

The quiet grimaced through the door, then there was some more, slightly more careful, swishing.

'I know you're out there,' I said. 'If you don't need anything then please go away.'

'Fuck off,' someone said mildly after a moment's hesitation.

In all likelihood, it was one of the Italian restaurateurs from the late 1800s. You have to be careful with other Peoples. Some of them like to hang out outside your Translation Room. Sometimes they whisper 'Scandi whore' when you walk past, simply because during a staff night out, very early in your Solveig career, you made out with one of the Irish dock workers. It ruins the momentum of an entire day somewhat, makes it more difficult to stay in one place. The being Solveig curdles for hours.

I think the idea behind the spying is to catch other people being less than useful. Algot, Solveig's brother-in-law, says he's seen this Italian guy arriving way too early for his own shift so that he can stand around and listen in on what I'm up to in there. Algot heard that he spends his own Translation Room listening to a recording of his grandfather yelling happily that the fascists are returning, over and over again. If he starts spreading rumours about what I do in mine, Algot says, I can always drop a mention about the fascist tapes to Joanne Tarbuck. Algot dislikes all Italians but one, his girlfriend. In any case, I'm not sure Joanne Tarbuck would care.

I'd just sat down in my armchair today when I felt like throwing up again. The nausea hatched through my jaws. I thought: this is what 'sick with worry' feels like, it's here, a body-fart, a falling

      handlöst   handlessly

through surfaces, levels, floors, and all the rubbish heaps. People are sick with worry all the time, though, and it helped to remember this, to hold hands with everyone else who's ever been sick with worry. There are millions. I just didn't know if it was you I was worried about, or what might happen to you when I'm not around. In the end, I managed not to actually be sick. Thinking about it, the English turn of phrase makes no sense, because it's surely when a person vomits that the sickness leaves them, once it's on the floor or on some other surface. At this point, they stop being sick.

I'd tucked my phone in under the waistband of my pants, underneath the Solveig shift. The pockets on it are meant for hammers and eggs, not in the same pocket, evidently, and not at the same time. Any of the times I checked it, you might have texted a return to normal proceedings:

Did you know that Trump was called Flat Top by his friends?

or

Holy shit, there are over a hundred uncontacted indigenous tribes around the world.

or

Want to go out for something to bottle?

Perhaps ask me to pick up some beers on the way home.

I didn't realise my phone had slipped out onto the chair until later, when I sneaked behind the East Bu dwelling-house at lunch time to check it again. There were two magpies eyeing up the same discarded keep-cup, waiting for the other to attack first. We're paid for our lunch hours so that we'll stick to our native languages even when we're eating. The paying public is easily disappointed — a £20 entrance ticket is supposed to buy you more than half-arsed multilingualism. Authenticity is such a deity around here.

Joanne Tarbuck was having lunch in her office when I knocked on her door. She became team leader long before I started and still hasn't unpacked all her boxes. She says she loves it here, of course. The boxes may just contain secret pets, like a dozen stick insects. She carefully opened the door with a string of cheese bridging the gap between her mouth and a slice of pizza, expecting an assault team.

'Hej!' I said.

'Oh crap,' Joanne Tarbuck said and looked up and down the corridor.

There was no one around to interpret.

'What is it?' she said. 'Wait! Don't answer that. Of course, don't answer that. Jesus, *Kirsten*.'

52

She'd managed to drag almost the entire layer of cheese from the pizza and into her mouth in one clean carpet-sweep, which meant we had to wait until she'd finished chewing. It took a long time.

'Det kommer en gammal	'There's an old person
människa uppför	coming up the stairs,'
trappan,'	
I said.	

On my way up from the Royal Palace entrance I'd walked past a question-mark-shaped woman holding a traffic cone. She was making her way up the stairs, stopping every couple of steps to reach out and touch the walls, closely examining the bricks and sniffing them. She did not seem out of breath — I walked slowly after her to check in case she collapsed. Now she was emerging at the end of the corridor. She stopped at the first office door and sniffed that, too.

'It's Dave Boyle's aunt,' said Joanne Tarbuck and turned back to me.

Dave Boyle is the team leader for the Irish dock workers.

'Jag lämnade min telefon	'I left my phone in my
i mitt översättningsrum,'	Translation Room,'
I said.	

'For Christ's sake,' said Joanne Tarbuck. 'You can't stand out here. Let me call someone.'

Then she went inside and closed the door behind her, leaving me standing out there.

Waiting for her to come back out, I made my face look non-understanding. It's a bit like pretending you haven't seen the use-by date on a yoghurt, because it still looks okay, when you shovel it into your mouth. It's like the face people fall into the second before they're approached by someone asking them for money for a night's shelter, just a couple of pounds is all that's missing. It took me the whole of my first year to get the hang of the non-understanding face. At the beginning, everyone flinches and turns their heads as if English was meant for them, too, as if this were their story.

The old woman was walking a few steps again, and then stopping, waiting for imaginary tiny animals to pass by safely in front of her feet. Joanne Tarbuck motioned for me to hurry inside and slammed the door behind us. Her office was not as massive as I remembered it; it was boiling.

'There's nothing I can do,' she said. 'The windows.'

She was grateful for those windows, she said.

The only other time I've ever been inside Joanne Tarbuck's office was on my first day, when she explained how out there, I would be Kristin (or Kirsten, or Karen) and in here I would be Solveig. She insisted that this was not to be seen as acting by any means. I was relieved — my parents are actors and that was never the plan. The plan was to only have this job through university.

We both turned our noses to the window, like fish to a surface, until Sigurd knocked on the door a whole five minutes later. He's Solveig's husband. They came together across the sea along with Ingrid, his mother, and Algot, his brother, and their father, Einar, who later died from a bad aim, planting an axe in his own foot. On Sundays Sigurd doesn't start until one, so thankfully he hadn't been to his Translation Room yet. Sigurd wasn't yet Sigurd, he was Niklas, and Joanne Tarbuck could use him to translate from English to Norwegian and from Swedish to English between us. We sat down in front of her desk.

'Jag glömde min telefon i   'I forgot my phone in my
mitt översättningsrum,'   Translation Room,'
I said again.

'She forgot her phone in her Translation Room,' Sigurd said.

'You're not supposed to have phones in Translation Rooms,' said Joanne Tarbuck.

'Det är inte meningen att   'You're not supposed to pay
du ska betala så lite i skatt,' so little in taxes,'
I said.

Niklas didn't translate this and I regretted saying it. I've begun to think of Joanne Tarbuck as sitting on top of a lot of things.

Niklas said, in Norwegian: 'You're not supposed to have a phone in your cupboard.'

I'm much better at understanding the Norwegians nowadays. During my first couple of summers it was tough. We were all supposed to be family, love each other very much, and be prepared to drown for each other crossing endless seas, but my Norwegian was abysmal.

'What's a "skap"?' said Joanne Tarbuck. 'That doesn't sound like it means Translation Room.'

'Oh it does,' said Sigurd. 'It's the closest we have.'

I think you'd like Sigurd. At least I don't think you'd think he was a twott.

I opened my mouth. Little hairs over Joanne Tarbuck's head fluttered and I said,

'Jag måste få tag på min pojkvän så att jag kan tala om för honom att jag har en tid hos barnmorskan i eftermiddag. Jag är tio, kanske elva veckor gravid och har inte varit hos läkaren ännu.'	'I have to get hold of my boyfriend so that I can let him know I have an appointment with the midwife this afternoon. I'm ten, maybe eleven, weeks pregnant and I haven't been to the doctor's yet.'

If you'd heard this you would have said: 'Fuck sake, K, you're not the first one this has happened to.'

You would never have said that. But you would have found it unnecessary.

Also, it wasn't true. I said it because the opportunity presented itself, for someone else to say it for me. As for Niklas, he could just excuse himself out of it, if he thought it was too sensitive a subject.

The surprise in his face went 'pft' and then it was all gone. He's a real actor, outside of work. He turned back to Joanne Tarbuck, who was looking at us and at her computer screen at the same time, even the hairs on her forearms wanting to wrap up the situation all by themselves. I heard she was a hand model for a while, before she became our team leader.

Niklas leant forward, interlacing his fingers on his knee and said, 'She needs to check in on her boyfriend because he's at home with a chest infection. She wants him to go to A&E this afternoon because he's had this for ten, maybe eleven, weeks and he hasn't been to see a doctor yet.'

Just that. Wow, the ficking speed of him.

'Don't let them give him antibiotics,' said Joanne Tarbuck. 'We're an inch away from a superbug and people keep popping antibiotics like they're cough-sweets.'

She sighed so hard she must have used up more than her fair share of the oxygen in the room.

'Pet,' she said, 'there's an emergency phone, yes?'

'There is,' I said. 'Hard to tell what kind of emergencies it's for.'

'Kirsten!' she said and touched her finger to her lips.

In spite of my transgression, she had someone fetch my phone and even left me with it for five minutes in her office to make the call, all alone with the photographs of her son and her diploma from an Open University Tourism Management course. Her mints. I called you, but you didn't pick up. Then there was a text:

| 'Varför du inte berätta | 'Why you not tell broken |
| trasig toa? | toilet?' |

Just after I left for work, I'd called the landlord to say there was something coming out of our toilet. I told him it was the colour of wine gums. He said he'd send someone over. I wanted you to be forced to interrupt yourself and improvise. Who knew the problem with the loo really was back? I spent the remaining two minutes in Joanne Tarbuck's office refreshing my text inbox, swiping and swiping it again until the screen became greasy. I looked at my hands, but they seemed clean. Joanne Tarbuck told

57

Niklas to hurry off quickly and head to his Translation Room so as to avoid any additional breakage of language barriers. I heard him ask why there hadn't yet been an announcement about tomorrow's Parade and she lowered her voice to answer.

Even if he'd translated what I'd said, she might still have said the thing about antibiotics. Nothing impresses me quite like a quick decision. It was nothing to do with him; he didn't have to get involved.

The old lady turned out to be Joanne Tarbuck's mother. Ingrid said so when I got back to the dwelling-house and mentioned to Algot that she'd been up there, inspecting surfaces like a small but relentless workforce. She's got Alzheimer's and has taken to showing up at the Castle looking for Joanne Tarbuck. The ticket-office people let her in to wander around the exhibitions because she used to have a great historical interest and because she's Joanne Tarbuck's mother. Ingrid has been at the Castle the longest out of everyone at East Bu. She likes clearing up mysteries and imparting unique information. Algot has to translate everything she says to me as she speaks Icelandic and I really don't. She understands most of what I say in Swedish, though, and there's something so unequal about this that sometimes when I'm standing next to her, I find something to step up on so that I can see the top of her head. Sometimes Algot is also just too tired to translate. He pretends he's always eating.

After work, when I was almost by the bridges, I heard someone close behind me declining a Fringe-show flyer. 'I live here, but thank you very much,' they said so very politely. It was just lovely — both decisive and kind — which is why I turned around and realised that the voice belonged to Niklas. I've only seen him a few times outside of work. Once was at a pub and we ignored each other because sometimes it's just too much hassle to decide how to speak with no rules in place.

'Hi,' I said.

He walked up beside me.

'Getting the bus?' he said.

In English he sounded like he should be overweight.

'It's not like they can actually do anything,' he said. 'It's up to us what we speak when we're out here. They're only trying to get people to go "above and beyond".'

He did the inverted commas at a level with his own ears. He looked like he was defending himself from an attack.

'Extraordinary commitment, you know,' he said. 'It makes them wet themselves.'

'Algot and I went on a date once, during my first summer,' I confessed.

He said: 'So, are you pregnant or not?'

I told him no, that I was helping a friend who was doing some research into different company policies and zero-hour contracts.

'The messenger always gets entangled,' he said by way of excuse, 'and I'm a very private person.'

One of the things this job does to people is that it makes the first language you ever spoke, the one you asked for someone to wipe your arse in, feel like you're taking your work home with you. I wanted to know if Niklas felt the same way, but even that was too much work, at the end of a long day.

'She was saying something to you, about the Parade,' I said. 'We should have heard by now.'

'She said she had a good feeling about it.'

'I don't like Joanne Tarbuck having a good feeling about something. Is it to do with the cows?'

'She didn't say anything about cows.'

'What else?'

'She said management are still debating. So, they're announcing it tomorrow just before we head off. She tried to talk me into postponing my holiday.'

'The Irish won't like that,' I said. 'They want to prepare. Are you sure she's not planning to make me bring along the cows? She thinks they're furniture.'

'Look at the time,' Niklas said. 'I'm off to a dinner date. Ta det rolig.'

ta det rolig	take it easy
in Norwegian	
rolig	funny
in Swedish	

I know that 'rolig' means 'calm' or 'easy' in Norwegian and not 'funny', but whenever he says it, I still think he's accusing me of not being much fun.

We got on separate buses. Niklas has a skin condition which makes his left hand look half-peeled, like part of the moon, but he's never mentioned any discomfort. It's the kind of thing only children ask but we all want to know: are you sure it doesn't hurt?

In the Norse sagas, Sigurd is the dragon slayer. He eats the dragon's heart and learns how to understand the language of birds. It's not really 'learning' though, is it? He simply gulps down a piece of meat, then magically understands the cawing and the tweeting. It's a carnal shortcut. The infamous 'blood eagle' is another one of those stories, which picked up celebrity status and ran away with it. The 'blood eagle' was supposedly a punishment during which the victim's ribs were broken off and the lungs pulled out through the back to resemble wings. But see, it could also have meant carving the shape of an eagle into the victim's back, or it could have referred to a practice of leaving the deceased (killed using a much more straightforward method) to be eaten by eagles. All of this is in the translation.

Another of your emails is from the time before we moved into the flat, the day you cancelled our day-trip to Lindisfarne because of a cold and I told you that I doubted your work ethic. Ha. If I'd known how much of an insult that would be. Getting to the island and back across before the high tide looked like a safe enough mission for people who didn't know each other that well yet.

> Look, I was feeling bad about borrowing Lucas's car
> and then not using it, so I've just been out to hoover it.
> It was an absolute mess, crumbs even on the dashboard.
> Now it's crumb-free but full of my cold. I found an
> empty pack of bacon-flavoured crisps and some fake-
> meat Scotch eggs. Lucas says he's vegan. I sat down in

the back of his car to check the list of ingredients on
both wrappers, and their contents are indeed vegan,
both of them, but they're also trying so hard not to
be vegan that it pissed me off. Why doesn't he just eat
some fucking chickpeas? Then I felt bad again because
I don't even like bacon so what do I know.

Tonight, only a few hours ago, you said that I was crapping on
your clean floor. This is pretty much what you said, in other
words. Fick you for saying that even if using other words. It's
half four am and practically Monday already.

You wanted to watch a Bergman film. It's part of the learning
plan, under Swedish Cultural Giants. Oh, the jokes to be made,
but I didn't really get to them.

'You won't like them,' I said. 'They're way up themselves.'

'This crassness is interesting,' you said, 'on a Sunday.'

'*You're* a Sunday!' I said.

'I know!' you said.

I made you an arrangement of chips, tomatoes, and gherkins
on a plate in the pattern of some country's flag. You said gherkins
always reminded you of holidays in the car around Fife with your
mother. I realised that I've never actually seen a Bergman film to
the end and had to give in. Give up. I asked you what the difference
was between the two and you, holding up *The Virgin Spring* in one
hand and *The Seventh Seal* in the other, said that it was probably a
matter of religion. Up or in, a direction of spirituality.

'Both of these look like handfuls,' you said and looked very happy, like this was the whole point, to never have empty hands.

I think you were looking for a place called Sweden in this film, but *The Seventh Seal* was released in 1957 and it's set during the Crusades. One character is a disillusioned knight and another one is Death. People speak through their noses. Generally, there is very little Sweden in the film. I sat there with your legs like an old person's blanket over mine and hoped that you would forever be making mistakes about Sweden based on this. Possibly, you could start thinking Swedish people were prone to dancing.

'Det är jag som är döden,' you learnt to say, which the subtitles translate as 'I am death'.

Det är jag	It is I
som	who
är döden	am/is death

It is I and nobody else.

'Death is being defensive,' I explained. 'Like someone else had claimed to be death before.'

'Thank you,' you said again. 'That's actually really helpful.'

We continued watching. Max Von Sydow used to be so tall; such a jaw, too.

You said: 'You know what would be even more helpful?'

I was wishing that I did embroidery. I was trying to see the back of your socks as they sometimes have holes the size of the entire heel and you won't admit it.

'I thought we were watching this,' I said and paused it.

'Yeah but,' you said, 'but, K, you're —'

'What is that, Welsh? But-but.'

You moved a foot away from me, unpaused the film, and left the blanket in a bundle. We finished watching it in silence.

'What are any of these people doing?' you said.

For the next hour or so, as we washed dishes, found money to pay a bill, chased a silverfish, I kept trying to list things which would be genuinely helpful in the current climate. A good government. Time travel. I only ever got to two items at a time which doesn't make a list, and it wasn't even close to what you, as it turned out, actually had in mind:

'I've been watching Disney films, too,' you said. 'It's almost properly working.'

'Did you watch *Toy Story*?' I said. 'The boy in that makes me look behind my shoulder.'

'Thing is,' you said, 'by the time you come home I've come a really long way,' you said. 'Like there's a flow. It feels like progress.'

'That word,' I said. 'Was it always that horrible?'

You pulled your left leg way back, diagonally on the carpet, and stretched. It looked unusual. I could feel it being a good thing for you. Then you wrote one more Post-it note and put it on the inside of the front door. It said DÄR UTE. Out there.

Soon after that, you explained how, according to research, language learning really does work best when you isolate yourself inside it, exposing yourself only to the language you're trying to learn.

'These Finnish kids, right? They have a system. They speak Finnish at school and Swedish in the home. That's the language bath, complete immersion.'

Tall Azif downstairs had just put on some Leonard Cohen.

'But the thing is,' you said, 'the tricky thing is that you come home.'

We looked not at each other.

'Holy fick,' I said.

'That's not what I meant.'

'I am the thing that *interrupts* you?'

'No! Jesus, Kristin. I just want you to help me, if you could, by speaking Swedish to me. Only Swedish. It would make such a difference, and you just refuse to help. It's like scrubbing the floor and then you come home and walk on it.'

'Maybe you don't want me to come home at all.'

'I told you, that's not what I meant,' you said.

'Well there you go,' I said. 'There is a *meant* after all.'

'What?'

'Your book,' I said. 'The one you were reading. You tell me things and I remember them.'

Since this morning there's been a dead slug on the windowsill in the bathroom. I suggested we take care of it for all of eternity.

'Fucking hell,' you said and stared at the ceiling. 'I can't hear myself think with him playing that!'

It sounded like a lovely evening down there. Maybe someone was shaving their legs.

'Do you not want me to speak to you?' I said. 'Is that actually what this is?'

'Kristin,' you said. 'Du sabotagar.'

'That's not a word. It's like saying "saboting".'

There was a new Post-it note on the map of Europe, across Poland. It said: 'All of this was Sweden.'

'And this,' I said. 'You're celebrating imperialism now.'

You turned around slowly, interlacing your fingers.

'Vad vill du göra?'   'What do you want to do?' you said.

You said it incredibly well, damn it.

'We could call the slug Slimy Sluggerson,' I said. 'Miss Viscosity RIP?'

'You pretend like nothing's happening,' you said. 'You won't *prepare*.'

'But there's no need! Not yet.'

'That's the kind of thing someone says who doesn't read the news every day. You're being so selfish.'

'You used to like Leonard Cohen,' I said.

I went for a walk after that.

I went down to Newhaven and the lighthouse. With only a few days to go before the festivals kick off, people are already spilling into every gap in the city. I tried to work up the courage to address a flyer-giver just like Niklas did earlier but instead I just stood there gaping at the poor girl, mouth much like a goldfish. They were all toasting each other for having discovered Edinburgh for the first time. Obviously, I don't want them all to stay, but maybe me thinking that means it's okay for other people to not want me to stay, so there you go.

The pier itself was empty. Speaking of staying, it looked like people weren't aware that it's fine to go out there. Local knowledge, I thought, hogging it. The two windows high up on the lighthouse tower made it look like a face with eyes too far apart and a flat cap. I climbed up onto the pier railings.

When I was younger, probably until very recently, I used to weigh the bad and the good things that happened, to me and others, against each other all the time, as if someone had raised me on karma.

'Om mamma får rollen på
Dramaten kanske mormor
dör. Är det värt att
mamma får rollen om det
betyder att mormor dör.
Mamma kommer gråta
i flera år om hon inte får
den där rollen.'

'If Mum gets the role at
Dramaten maybe Grandma
will die. Is it worth Mum
getting the role if it means
that Grandma will die?
Mum will cry for years if she
doesn't get that role.'

That was aged nine. Mormor died anyway. Mum cried for years. Every time something great happened, there was the immediate threat of something absolutely gross following on directly afterward, but not because of gravity or the stock market. I think it was balance, which is different.

'Om vi åker och badar idag
kanske vi inte går på bio
på fredag. Om Frankrike
slutar testa atomvapen
kanske pappa blir sjuk.'

'If we go swimming today
we might not go to the
cinema on Friday. If France
stops testing atomic weapons,
perhaps my dad will get sick.'

67

'Om vi överlever detta   'If we survive this we might
kanske vi aldrig är oss   never be ourselves again.'
själva igen.'

We never believe we have that kind of power anymore, that our nerves are tied up with everyone else's endings. Cause and effect did not stand in line then, they spilt and they burst to the sides. If one shoe falls off and bobs away in the direction of Fife, then we will all be allowed to stay in the country. If I lose both shoes (which would really only happen if I took them off and threw them in the water) then we'll both learn to take care. If one of us gets very sick, then the other will live to save something beautiful, something great.

Over on the shore, there was a surprisingly elegant lady looking at me. She wore a fascinator. I tried to decide whether to wave or not to wave, whatever wouldn't make her think I was about to jump, although jumping from there you'd only get wet. I remained on the railings for a while, balancing on my sit bones on the metal, a being-perched more than a perching, by the feel of it. I thought of those hideous photos of chickens in overpopulated coops. It was only me there, but still like a being-crowded. I tried to decide whether to go home now or wait for another ten minutes. Walking home I came across the same girl giving away flyers and she gave me another, identical, one. I tried to decide whether or not to take it.

When I came back, you were scrubbing the blackboard-schedule clean. I sat down on the floor and watched you start again with tomorrow's itinerary. When you were done, you came over. You took hold of my knees. I grabbed your wrists. Your eyelashes clipped, some congealed eye-goo on the left and the stubble hopping back and forth over your jaws. It will take a lot for it to go grey, but we don't know how grey, because of adoptions, because you might catch a disease of the hair follicles, why not? Because we, as we, may not be around that long. Your phone was ringing and when you didn't pick up, they left a cough instead of a message.

'What about all of them?' I said. 'Are you going to speak Swedish to them as well?'

'I've made arrangements,' you said. 'My mum thinks I'm camping.'

'Arrangements,' I said.

'Just until I'm back at work or if you really need me.'

Which would mean what exactly?

'I just think it will work so much better that way,' you said. 'Completely.'

At about eleven pm I set about looking up all the old school friends I could find online to check if any of them had died or become neo-Nazis. You were getting ready for bed.

'Just one last thing,' you said. 'I need to order a new bucket but I don't want to read stuff in English, could you do it for me?'

'Is it for the mouse in the freezer?'

'Hans namn aaaarr Ernie.'   'His name is Ernie.'

'No,' I said. 'We're not naming anything else after your mum's exes. No way are we doing that.'

You got into bed, pulled the covers up, looked at me as I rummaged, and said:

'Jag är ledsen.'

You waited. You pulled back the covers on my side and arranged it all for me to get in.

'Exactly for what?' I said.

'Jag är ledsen,' you said. 'For the ambush.'

Here are two of the ways people apologise in Swedish.

förlåt	forgive
för	fore
låt	let/give but also 'song'
Then there's:	
jag är ledsen	I am sorry
but also	I am sad

Maybe if you'd gone with 'Förlåt mig' instead of 'I am sad' I wouldn't have said, 'That's okay', and got into bed.

I wouldn't have spent the rest of the night awake.

Förlåt mig is different. Förlåt mig pushes the onus onto the forgiver to step up, to do the work. 'I am sad,' though. That's a whole other movement, another look. You're sad about so many things. At least there's work to be done in that: 'I'm sad.'

IN HERE

Monday

Some afternoon, way back, I asked you about your first memory, the way new people do when they're wanting — desperate nutters — to get to the bottom of other new people. I dislike that we've been just those kinds of people.

> You know I don't think I have one? There's this picture I remember, of a horse, a plastic rocking horse with real eyelashes, and me holding a plastic cup at a plastic table, really wanting to grab the weird eyelashes. For a long time, I thought this was my first memory, but then when I was about fourteen my mum gave me a picture she had of me in the orphanage and it was the exact same thing. The weird eyelashes. Turned out that I'd seen it before because she kept it in a drawer I used to look through when she wasn't home. There's a massive gap after the horse memory. Huge. Like across to Scotland and aged six or seven. So, I don't think that's it.

I don't know if you remember that Hogmanay in fourth year when you were working at that newsagent's, and we went to a party in some posh student's parents' flat. A guy asked us if we'd ever been to South America, only so that he could talk about his gap year. You looked at him like he was this incredibly interesting person, like you were a politician, angling for his liking, and said that no, unfortunately you had not been there, no.

I spoke to my parents and they told me that a cousin of mine, who's ten years older than I am, has just announced that she's 'finally' having a baby. They've been through two rounds of IVF treatments, my parents said to me, twice. I asked them how they know what she's having. How can they be sure she's not having an accident or a jellyfish? Nothing stays a baby for long. They become people who will become victims, or patients, or yoga teachers, if there are still yoga teachers in twenty years' time. People do not *have* babies, they have projects.

'Why does your generation think it owns Great Danger?' my dad said.

My mum began talking about Sweden's stock of paracetamol during the Cold War. The country could easily have been self-sufficient for six months at the time. 'Not so anymore,' she said. 'They dismantled our defences.'

I said I couldn't speak for the other millions of my generation, especially those in Bangladesh, but that I, for one, don't watch the news anymore.

'What about Ciaran,' my mum asked. 'When we met, he struck me as so well informed.'

I said that you still are, which is a lie. You're only watching the news in Swedish this week, and getting a minimal portion

74

of anything happening. This seems to make you more at ease with time passing.

Are you having fun? People do say that learning languages is great fun. According to an online etymology encyclopaedia, the word fun entered the English language in the 1680s:

fun   cheat/hoax
Its origin may be found in the Middle English word
fonnen   befool
What does that say about having fun?
You wrote me once, about fun:

> People who almost die for fun are fucking stupid.
> They throw themselves off cliffs and then they laugh at
> lemmings? I do know lemming suicides aren't real, by
> the way. My pal Nadine is going to America to jump
> off a plane next summer, attached to her cousin, whom
> she has a crush on. I've told her she might throw up
> in mid-air and then where will they be, romantically
> speaking? Nadine has cancer but it's not terminal
> cancer. I keep telling her that, too, but she doesn't hear
> the difference.

You had a nosebleed this morning, right after you sat up in bed and counted flawlessly, in Swedish, from one to fifteen. Were you dreaming of an army? I pretended it hadn't woken me up. I've stopped correcting your pronunciation because I know that's what you want me to do.

Speaking again about fun. VIKINGS. Scandinavian folk. Long hair and longer boats.

We are examples, Joanne Tarbuck says, here to symbolise one of the many Peoples who made Scotland what it is, and to celebrate its rich cultural multiplicity. There's a quiet war raging between Joanne Tarbuck and Ingrid about our entertainment value. Joanne Tarbuck claims that Ingrid is on a mission to throw the Norse into oblivion and Ingrid says she, a retired archaeologist who only stays working at the Castle to gain access to the library for the sake of the book she's writing, is championing historical accuracy. Joanne Tarbuck argues that people like seeing things burn. Ingrid points out that if you look at the actual archaeological finds, funeral pyres were not that common on the Northern Isles, possibly due to the lack of timber. But, Joanne Tarbuck says, it looks *intense*, and it also pays Ingrid's wages so that she can go back to Iceland and visit her grandchildren every six months, which the real Norse would probably not have done. So, which does she prefer?

The four of us live in a reconstructed roughly tenth-century dwelling-house squeezed in, beams and dirt floor and all, on Drury's Battery, behind what used to be the POW museum at the back of the Castle. Right next to it, there's a small byre with the cows in it. When the museum first opened, the Vikings used to live in a proper longhouse, the kind people think of if they ever think of how Vikings lived and not just how they killed, until Ingrid bombarded management with scientific evidence that longhouses were a later phenomenon. During our time, the farmhouses were most likely separate from the dwelling-houses. The byre allowed for cows, which is how Björn Skifs and Lady Gaga arrived.

'We could all have been sharing a room,' I say to them and they glance at anything but the human in the room.

The hair pins are also Ingrid's doing. When people think about Vikings, especially Viking women (which is, of course, in itself problematic as Viking was a job and not very common among women, although a number of articles challenge this view), they don't generally think of them wearing headscarves. Management insisted they were grateful when Ingrid informed them about the hair pin, found in several female graves on Orkney and Shetland. Headscarves were promptly introduced for the sake of authenticity. Sometimes you can smell the disappointment in the doorway to the dwelling-house before the tourist comes in: the surprise at how poor everything looks. How medieval. Headscarves are the opposite of free, which is the same as sexy, both of which Vikings should be. Free and sexy. Sometimes bloody, too. Free, sexy, and bloody.

Ingrid has just once during her employment been invited as an expert to a management meeting.

'What about the language?' she said.

The meeting had gone really well until then.

'They spoke Old Norse, not Swedish and Norwegian.'

Ingrid was thanked and not invited to any further meetings.

When I first started working as Solveig, Joanne Tarbuck told me she didn't believe in documentaries. This was about working up

77

some atmosphere, getting people to *imagine* things.

'Like ghosts?' I said.

'If you want to take it in that direction,' she said.

She managed to find a film, somewhere in the depths online, called

| *Sigurd och Solveig: över berg* | *Sigurd and Solveig: over* |
| *och hav* | *mountain and sea* |

It's from 1972. There are hundreds of Viking films in English, but surprisingly few in Swedish. *Sigurd and Solveig* is about a family from somewhere in Norway in the 900s who leave their lives behind to find a better home across the sea in Britain. Even the light, a very beige orange, looks typical of the seventies. Solveig's hair is so big the wind clearly has nothing to do with it. She cries a lot. Sigurd bellows and broods. She does look a bit like I do, in her clothes, and I look a bit like she does in the indoor scenes, when it's difficult to see their faces and they're all having serious conversations about how the gods might react. When I mentioned the film to my parents, they went very quiet.

'Darling, have you ever watched the *whole* film?'

I looked it up. After the third sex scene I went back to my assigned twenty minutes and have stuck with that since. There was so much cloth being thrown.

The tower room is the size of about half our lounge. From the angle of my armchair, the tiny cupboard in the corner looks like it has both eyes and a mouth with something critical to say, something no one's ever paid attention to. The space smells

78

mostly like dust, and sometimes like a fishmonger, which now makes me think of the story my dad told me about a seal on the west coast of Sweden. That seal swam all the way into the fishmonger's during a flooding last year. When I told you about this, I remember you saying, 'They have nowhere else to go.'

Just before the film clip ended today, I got off my chair and onto the floor, to do ten non-sit-ups — contracting everything but lifting nothing. I was trying to find out where I end, and I'm perfectly aware that an actual pregnant person doesn't think sheet like that. I've always found it tricky, this being a body. I can talk or listen to people talking about bodies all day long (take the month you spent studying joints, the gut month, and the ear month, all the new words these brought with them), but it's not the same as being in one, unrelentingly and with no way out. If you and I had met at a different point in our lives, we wouldn't have had English to meet in. There would be no Bobe or Squirrel McCamp because I didn't learn English until I was twelve and got into BBC documentaries about the Plantagenets in a big way. I read and re-read about beheadings and I ate dill and sour cream crisps for lunch every day. You could have said 'hiya' and I would have said 'va?' and then we would have fled with our respective friends, inside our respective bodies, and that would have been it. Thank fick we didn't meet when I was twelve. I would only have seen your body. I'd love to know what that would have been like.

There were Swedes down at East Bu today, which doesn't happen very often. They tend to go more for other Peoples when on holiday. Sometimes they're interested in the Norse artefacts up at the Palace, but most often they just walk along to the square outside the National War Museum, where the Irish are always preparing to sail. These two had most likely ended up there by accident. They were making out behind the byre. I was brushing Lady Gaga between her ears, where nobody else is allowed to touch her.

'They didn't even speak Swedish back then,' one of the Swedes said.

'Britter hör väl ingen   'Brits don't hear the
skillnad,'   difference,'

said the other. Then it was all sounds of tissue and of urgency.

'Väl' is a very wee word, and hard to translate. It can mean 'well' but also 'probably'. There's definitely a difference, in any case, between 'Brits don't hear the difference' and 'Brits väl don't hear the difference'. The 'väl' in the latter leaves a space for doubt to be smuggled in.

du älskar mig väl   you do love me

Here, the väl is a question mark and someone needs to have a long hard look at themselves.

When the Swedes had gone, Algot came into the byre to ask me where Sigurd was. He wasn't having a good hair day, which puts him in a bad mood. He'd also forgotten that this is Sigurd's week off. Summer is raiding time anyway, so part of the story is that Sigurd is away down south. In the *Solveig and Sigurd* film, Algot is the one out and about slashing. In the twenty minutes I've watched, they bring him back bleeding twice. Film Solveig is a very skilled wound-dresser and forehead-wiper.

'They're just about to announce the Parade,' said Algot.

'It's almost half ten,' I said. 'The Irish must be fuming.'

The parade usually starts at midday. The Irish are always really keen.

Algot said, 'Did I tell you that I don't mind anymore? Since I started practising mindfulness, they can't touch me.'

I went over to Björn Skifs whose eyelids seemed inflamed. Her knees reminded me of how the purpose of knees is really to hold two sticks together, so there. I went over a few excuses for not having finished brushing her, but they all sounded like a person speaking to an animal and in the end, I couldn't bring myself to say anything to her. Algot says it's typically Swedish to assume people know about our local celebrities. Björn Skifs is a seventies Swedish pop singer, but the reason I chose that name was the opposite: so that no one else would accidentally say it and have her come to them.

Algot sat down on his favourite part of the bench, where there are fewer public particles, he says.

'Actually, Joanne Tarbuck popped in earlier and said it was really close this year. The Italians must have come up with something. Do you think she would be a good eyewitness in a crime investigation?'

'Why the Italians?' I said.

'They can do pasta over and over again,' said Algot. 'Just different kinds. They should do that and they'd be sorted every single year.'

He then went to hide behind the byre for a while to text his Italian girlfriend. There's a great view there over the Pentlands which we all go to for a little breathing, a tantrum, hand over mouth. Pentland is a Norse word, too:

Pentland   Pictland   land of the Picts

They still hadn't said anything about the cows, and at eleven the farmer from North Berwick came to take them to their pasture. Every other day they get to go away for a few hours to stretch their legs and reduce the risk of lameness.

We were rounded up on Argyle Battery to listen to the announcement. It wasn't raining, but the Firth was spitting up salt, hardly there enough to prove it. I had to concentrate to properly get my

väderstreck   weatherlines

compass points   kompasspunkter

in order, fishing scraps and memories out of the postcard down there.

When it creeps up the slopes of Castle rock, Edinburgh sometimes hits me right on the nose. Every time, it's like I'm asked to choose it again, and always for the first time. Most often I just stand there, for minutes, like someone who forgot why she came into a room. Anyone talks to you about a place and you'll tell them what the indigenous species are and why there is a certain weather based on the position of the mountains. You talk about wood and feral pigeons, also about chaffinches. I just see pigeons. What makes the place for me is the basement flat in Stockbridge we stood outside of for twenty minutes that time, before we found out the party had been cancelled. The curry place where the chana made you hallucinate. The zoo is down there, and I still suspect the penguins may well enjoy their parade. Whenever I splurge about the sexiness of the city, you tell me that it's big, outrageously polluted and polluting, and I always think that's fine to say that about anywhere else, but not about this city, which took me in and made me breakfast.

In hindsight: if I'd had some forethought, I would first have established a longer relationship with the city independently of you, possibly through cycling, community volunteering, or drinking, bursting through the tarmac and into someone's life. I should have waited six months or so before asking you out. Even the flat. I've started thinking about it as yours more than ours, even though I can hear you less and less in it.

So, there we all were. The Irish dock workers, the Italian entertainers and restaurateurs, the Polish and the Lithuanian miners, the French aristocracy, and, over on the edge, the maintenance and hospitality staff looking on it all, like it was more than ridiculous and like they wouldn't say no if invited. This announcement, once a year, is one of very few exceptions to the rule of non-understanding. It would be way too expensive to get in interpreters for every language just for the one meeting. I had a look but couldn't see Barbara. I did spot her sister though, who's quite big. Barbara could have been standing behind her. Both Algot and Ingrid were looking over at the Italians, the Italians were only speaking to each other. How special did they think today was? One of them yawned. Beyond all of that, the tourists were pissing themselves with excitement.

Dave Boyle used a box between two of the cannons to stand on. He's very small and has dusty hair that looks like it will disintegrate in your hand, glasses so square they remind me of the computer games I used to play when I was little and my parents were away on tour.

'We won't have time to go back and change,' Algot said.

Ingrid giggled and elbowed him.

'You want to get ready for your fans,' I said, but not as a question. This always riles him up.

'You don't look believable,' he said to me.

A French guy put his hands over his friend's eyes. They seemed to have a game going. One of the Polish reached up to the sky and a few people followed his gaze but saw nothing except a seagull.

'Well then,' Dave Boyle said and cleared his throat. 'So, this year, it was a tricky one wasn't it?'

The rest of management, clustered by his side, nodded. Joanne Tarbuck wasn't there, we noted. We should probably have noticed earlier that Joanne Tarbuck wasn't there, and gone to haul her out of her ficking office.

'We had some really convincing last-minute submissions,' Dave Boyle said. 'I mean who knew that Copernicus was Polish? I certainly didn't.'

'Kevin knew!' someone shouted.

'But then again, it needs to have been a contribution to

Scotland, specifically. Copernicus, as far as we have been able to ascertain, didn't live in Scotland, so I'm afraid that submission fell short. Jolly good suggestion, though.'

Ingrid was scraping the ground with the toe of one of her shoes.

'So,' Dave Boyle continued. 'Dear colleagues, this year we'll be celebrating a contribution which we can all enjoy on a daily basis right here in this city. It's become very popular lately, with new Swedish cafes popping up every month it seems. It's not quite coffee and it's not quite tea. It can be cake and it can be a biscuit, too, I'm told! It's a whole cultural phenomenon, of togetherness if you will.'

'Oh bleurg,' Algot said.

'You'll have seen the T-shirts the staff wear in the cafes. Does anyone know what they say?'

It was quiet except for Ingrid's toe-scraping.

'No one? No?'

'He's not really that short, when you're actually looking at him,' Algot said.

'Fika!' Dave Boyle shouted.

Oh sheet. Ficking coffee memories flying everywhere; my mum, grandparents, a graffiti unicorn.

'Swedish "fika"! Am I saying it right, folks?'

I could have sworn that someone had just dropped something and I dove toward it, spent a good minute around Ingrid's feet. Algot waved at Dave Boyle and then lowered his

85

hand to give him the finger.

'I didn't do anything but I'm sorry,' I said to Ingrid's calves.

'The People heading up the Parade this year will be the Vikings! A round of applause for the Vikings. Very nice, that. Fika. Who doesn't like a coffee break?'

Their stares almost had a sound, they were so intimate.

Once that was done, everyone ran back to their areas to get accessories. We had fifteen minutes before the Parade was meant to begin. Normally, Algot likes at least half an hour to work up the mood. Our fingers fumbled for beads, for shields and swords. The other two didn't say a word to me during the entire time.

'Look at you,' I said. 'Assuming.'

They still didn't say anything. Algot spent several minutes scrubbing a penny-sized area of his shield only to sneeze on it and glare at me again. Ingrid left to wait outside, taking her völva staff. The middle bit is curved with five branches creating the shape of a small seedpod between them. They come together at the top where she holds it to cast spells. Officially, she objects to it. It's modelled on a staff found in Sweden — so geographically the wrong kind of Norse, really, a Norse from the wrong place. I fastened my brooches. The way to make them look real and heavy is to picture that you're being pulled down by your collar bones, down and down as much as you can toward your knees. Get a real bend in, if you can. Make them believe you're about to keel over.

My mother used to teach drama to kids with concentration

difficulties in the community hall and I'd go and do my homework in the cafe after school.

'Ta en fika,'   'Have a fika,'

she used to say, 'I'll be done in no time.'

When she talked about fika, she always meant black coffee from the pot brewed that morning.

'I'm eight,' I said.

'Mozart wrote his first piece at the age of eight,' she said, but she didn't mean I was doing badly.

There was a graffiti unicorn on one of the walls with huge balls which kept reappearing whenever the staff painted over them.

'That right there,' you said when I told you that story, 'is the origin story of an addict.'

The Peoples lined up on the esplanade, with us at the very front. It was like the head of a big animal had been cut off and tada! There we were, a very small, rigid neck. The Italians still seemed excited about it. One of them was doing handstands. When I started suspecting she was trying to fall on me I tried to think about what you said after an incident with a wanker police officer once, about not expecting the worst from people.

'Where the hell is Joanne Tarbuck?' Algot said.

'Incognito,' I said.

During last year's Parade she ran all the way along the edges of the Mile, popping up and down behind the shoulders of spectators to take pictures for the website and to make sure we were actively but non-verbally interacting with the public. I waved to a little boy who started laughing. Then he immediately choked. The adult who was with him, a father or uncle with bad acne scars and an I HEART EDINBURGH T-shirt, looked at me and seemed to know so much about the things I've tried.

We set off, with the Italians providing the music. It was a whole other thing being at the front of the Parade. You could see the first few faces, the tourists stopping because something, *something* might be missed otherwise. Algot kept rolling his eyes. Ingrid pushed me forward. I told her she should be caring.

'It's the least you can do,' Algot whispered.

Then, as we emerged from the esplanade and down the close to the Royal Mile, there was a wave of cheering from the sides, hands clapping in their hundreds. This made Algot straighten up. After that the bagpipes got going and a few people started stomping with their feet, some even with their buggies.

'Jesus, the babies,' Algot said.

I thought about the dancing characters at the end of the Bergman film, hand in hand skipping up a hill. Possibly, you were re-watching it this very moment. No, mornings are for grammar. People were stopping to check us out and staying.

'Oh, why not then,' said Algot.

He held up his sword to an avalanche of cheering. Ingrid began to hum, quietly at first and then so loudly that it made a family of three who were about to pop into a cashmere shop turn around. Algot stepped a few feet ahead of the parade and held his sword higher, then he waved it from side to side. Ingrid was getting more and more into her humming, too. She'd never done her shamanic routine with that many spectators before.

By the time we'd passed Castle Street, we were all sharing the crowd like a drink. Oh fick, I thought, and took my scarf off. The first yell came shortly after that. Someone piped up from the back of the line:

'Show us your fika!' they shouted.

We all assumed we'd heard wrong, although we'd all heard the same thing. Ingrid was marching to my left, a step or so ahead of me, and she turned to look at me the second time it happened:

'It's just coffee and cake!' a woman yelled.

She sounded like she could be from somewhere around Leeds.

'I have no idea,' I said.

Ingrid stopped singing. Algot didn't seem to have heard it. He was falling to his knees and shielding himself from an imaginary eagle attack. People kept applauding and we got almost to George IV Bridge before the next salvo:

'You didn't invent feckin' coffee and cake!'

'We never said we did!' I shouted and this time Ingrid elbowed me.

It sounded like it was coming from nearby but when I turned to the Italians, they were all smiling. Their faces were so smooth they looked like they were all at church together. Algot turned around with his sword held up. All still, like that, for all anyone knew it could have cut through helmets, then it instantly began to wobble, a tired celery.

'Fika me in the arse!' someone yelled.

I stepped in a puddle of something that couldn't have been

water because it hasn't rained in days. It seeped into my true-to-life moccasins. Ingrid began to properly shriek now: *hiaaaaaaaa, wiaaaaaaaa*, she went and the tendons in her neck shot up like flag poles.

'Is she very ill?' I heard someone say.

'Suck my fika!' came from the right.

Ingrid whispered something to Algot, but with the music and the noise from the crowd, not a single word leaked out, at least not one of the few Icelandic ones I know, such as 'launahækkun'. It means 'pay rise'. I thought of how different mine and Ingrid's relationship would need to be for it to be normal for me to reach out and grab her hand. Would we have to start over again, or just get a little bit drunk? In Solveig's time holding hands was probably not something you did with your mother-in-law anyway, ever. If I were Solveig, the rules might have been clearer.

'I really promise that I really didn't do it,' I said and started walking faster.

I wonder what I would have called her, if she'd appreciated me bringing her a little something in the mornings or the other way around. If I were Solveig, public humiliation may have entailed a flogging or exile. If I were Solveig, I might have known what to do.

'K-meter,' you'd say if I told you what happened. 'In many parts of the world public humiliation still means flogging.'

'Do cows feel what's going on in each of their stomachs?' I'd say.

If we were saying much that mattered.

Brazil is one of the highest coffee-producing countries in the world and Sweden one of the most coffee-consuming. We did have something in common, right from the start. Except you detest coffee. It gives you horrendous farts and makes you say rude, two-syllabled things, especially to your mother and to people working on customer-care phone lines. You care so much about the old people that you always make sure you don't have coffee during a work shift, no matter how tired you get and how offended they are when they offer it to you and you say no.

'Aren't you Brazilian?' they say. 'Because I sure as hell wouldn't say no to a dram if it was offered such a long way from home. Haha.'

We still finished the Parade, went all the way down to Holyrood, made a loop around the Parliament pond, before heading back up again. The crowds thinned out toward the bottom of the Canongate, as did the shouting. Then it all started up again on the return leg. Because we were leading it, at least we were able to set the pace and we legged it. Normally the whole Parade takes forty-five minutes and this time it was all over in twenty. When we got back to East Bu Ingrid was so angry that she kicked the fake chicken out the door, just as one of the two real chickens we have was passing by, so that chicken hit chicken in mid-air. The only two things I could think were: so much right now has never happened before. And: the unicorn, I couldn't take my eyes off that unicorn. What I said was:

'Det var inte jag.'   'It wasn't me.'

Ingrid crossed her arms and mumbled at me.

'She says you obviously went behind her back and that's really cheap,' Algot said.

'Well,' I said, 'I'm sorry, but I think that says more about you. Or her. Both of you.'

'---- ---- her,' said Ingrid. 'I --------- not ----------- --- ------'

'She wants me to explain to you,' said Algot. 'That she thinks you're opportunistic.'

A person peeked in through the front door and shouted: 'Booo!'

'Someone something something,' Ingrid said.

'Cheap, ahistoric trend-fucking,' Algot translated.

'She didn't say that,' I protested. 'There's no way she said that, just look at her face.'

We stared at the dirt floor. There was the flash of a camera and an embarrassed giggle in the doorway, but the atmosphere in there must have smelt terrible and the tourist ran away without so much as a question about horns or no horns.

'I'm going up to talk to Joanne Tarbuck,' said Algot.

'Oh wow,' I said. 'Remember to bring her offerings.'

'So evident,' he said. 'So *very* evident that they waited till the last minute. That way we wouldn't have time to argue.'

I held up a brooch.

'You know,' I said. 'I. Don't. Care. About this shit.'

'Well, guess what,' said Algot and nodded toward Ingrid. 'She does.'

She had already begun to bake.

'Well,' I said. 'How do you plan to talk to Joanne Tarbuck in English at this time of day?'

Algot said she wasn't good at ignoring people for long, not when they were right there, with their feet in her office. He left, and I went on my lunch break.

My feet were starting to ache. The area on my hip where my phone was pressing against the skin had become hot and sweaty. Fluorescent Project, I thought and then I stopped thinking that, went back to the graffiti unicorn with the balls.

After preparing the next batch of dough, Ingrid began to tidy inside the dwelling-house. She was taking such longs steps I couldn't stay in there for long, and I spent the rest of my lunch break staring at the Pentlands behind the byre.

People get obsessed with the consistency of mountains. I'm using the word wrong, though. I always use that word wrong:

consistency as in   the firmness, the gliding, the sound when it falls

consistency as in   staying the same, itself

If I were Solveig, I might even have looked at these same hills. I might have thought that they weren't that different from hills back home and that they weren't safe, because of what they might do or what might come from them. There was a text from your mother.

'Hey love, do you know if there's something wrong with Ciaran's phone?'

'He's hiking,' I wrote. 'He's reinventing himself as a businessman.'

I deleted the last bit.

When I got back from lunch, Algot still had not returned from the office. In the meantime, Ingrid and I got on with cutting up some wood. With the more-regular-than-usual burnings of Einar, the dead father-in-law, we've been running out really quickly. After that, Ingrid sat down outside the dwelling-house to work on her latest steatite bowl. Steatite bowls have been found in Norse graves, especially on Shetland. Ingrid taught me how to carve them. We have a whole collection now, set up in a half-moon around the fire place but not for sale yet, as the handling of cash wouldn't look right. If people want to, they can use them for trying the bread or the porridge. I offered some bread to a guy in his late fifties who was walking around inspecting the house, bumping into things with his bag. I gestured for him to bake the bread himself over the fire. He looked at it and chuckled.

'No way, lady. No disrespect but who knows what you put in there.'

We both laughed.

'Gift?'   'Poison?'

I said.

He rolled his eyes and went to take some photos of Algot's armour. Interesting, that in Swedish the words for poison and for being married are the same:

jag är gift   I am poison

The things you learn from tourists.

'Thank you anyway,' said the guy without looking at me.

94

| 'Jag väntar mig inte det värsta av dig,' I said. | 'I don't expect the worst from you,' |

I went and sat down next to Ingrid outside the house. She had one of the East Bu flagons next to her on the cobbled stones. It kept getting knocked over when she worked, but she wouldn't put it away. It was confusing to see that kind of self-sabotage happening in real time. I wriggled my petticoat over my head and it got caught in one of the hair pins so that all I could hear for a good minute were loud Spanish voices. Someone had completely lost control of their children out there, and it felt like if I came out again something terrible would have happened to them — the fun day would have become a tragedy from one moment to another. It's like you say you feel in the mornings sometimes, when you open your eyes and, overnight, someone has royally ficked up again. It can't be taken back or away. If I were pregnant now, that is the 'out there' I'd be pregnant in. The kid continued laughing way beyond the point where it was sweet.

'You -------- ?' Ingrid said and yanked at my petticoat.

When I'd weaselled out of it, I saw that she was making a peace sign at a girl with a runny nose. The discharge was solidified, cracked; the girl was wearing a T-shirt with bears on it.

Ingrid handed over the flagon. Because she's always reminding the rest of us to drink more water, I took it and ended up with a mouthful of lukewarm white wine sloshing about in my mouth. I didn't spit it out and she laughed. She looked pleased. The child with the Niagara Falls of snot under her nose continued to stand there, waiting for what the woman with the dreadlocks and strange wooden stick would do next, which wasn't much. Ingrid elbowed me on the hip again, where my flask is usually tucked in.

'What?' I said and gave the flagon back. 'I don't do that anymore.'

She rolled her eyes and poured out the last few drops of wine between the cobbled stones. The liquid chose strange paths on its way downhill. Before I'd thought much about it, I said:

'Jag dricker inte just nu.   'I'm not drinking right now.

Jag är med barn,'   I am with child,'

'Ha!' said Ingrid, slapping me on the thigh.

At that point the kid finally got bored and ran away. Ingrid continued to polish her new bowl, pressing it into her ribs like she was trying to discern a pattern right down on the bottom. She couldn't have understood what I'd said. If she had, she would have taken me aside, ignored every rule, and explained, in English, the consequences of this or that course of action. She would have asked for a time-out.

'Solveig ------ mamma!' she said and absently took a shoe off to wiggle her toes.

I should stretch more at work. Stretching is good. We should massage each other's shoulders.

'What about Solveig?' I said. 'What are you saying?'

The same thing came out of her again: *Solveig. Mamma.*

Well now. That was something.

'Oh!' I said and stared at her hands.

Well. Why not? Why couldn't *she* be?

Ingrid's left hand curled around the staff and I looked at the three compressions on the side of it, where that fleshy part narrows into the little finger and stamps the skin with a bird's foot. For a while when I was a kid, we ran around telling all kinds of strangers how many children they'd have based on those folds of flesh, including old-age pensioners. Nearly everyone was destined for three children, it seemed. I told Ingrid that Solveig's pregnancy hadn't been Joanne Tarbuck's idea, but mine. I said the idea had come to me in the shower.

'Some of them did mean to colonise,' I said. 'You'd think they hurry up and procreate.'

We sat in silence for a while and in that time we carved a whole new bowl between us, passing it from her to me, from me to her and back.

They used to carve steatite bowls straight from the rock, shaping the bottom of the bowl upside-down and then severing it, like a wart growing on the stone's surface. If we were driving sharp tools into pieces of stone inside the museum, people would get hit by the splinters, so instead we're given chunks of dark wood to carve our bowls from. One of the signs on the board outside the dwelling-house explains the discrepancy and asks visitors to use their imagination, please.

'------- ------ -------- falskur magi?' said Ingrid and let out a little giggle.

I asked her to repeat it. The Bear Snot child was back,

97

holding a massive burger with the lettuce halfway out.

falskur	sounds like falsk
	which means false
magi	sounds like mage
	which means belly

I looked down at Solveig's belly, a mundane fall of shift and petticoat moving about, following suit, and then I could see it, the growing, the bounciness of it as something that would happen in there, with time. Ingrid laughed. She, too, was thinking about what Solveig would look like and finding it entertaining. She was getting used to the idea. I grabbed her flagon and drained the last drop of wine, just to make sure there was no doubt as to who was pregnant and who wasn't. The longer I looked down at my stomach, all wrapped in the Solveig clothes, the more chilled it seemed in there, the more possible, and the more like someone else's.

Not very long ago, Algot was trying to persuade Joanne Tarbuck to let him wear a fat suit to keep warm over the Christmas season. There's a lot of standing around and selling of mead in the cold around that time. The winters should make it easier to be Viking. There's something about hanging on and dealing with, withstanding, etc, etc, that comes with the package, but we're not doing much manual labour to keep us warm. Algot didn't get the suit because it wouldn't add to the value of the visitor experience. When he came back from the office today, he marched straight past us. We followed him inside the dwelling-house and waited as he drank some water, stared at the wall for a while, then kicked a sack of grain, then poured the rest of the water on top of the grain.

'You could piss on it,' I said. 'Just say the roof leaked again and they might give us insulation.'

'Fuck,' he said in very slow and deliberate English.

'Algot!' said Ingrid and put her hands, oddly, over her eyes.

'She did it,' he said, not in English. 'The Tarbuck. She came up with the coffee idea. She said we should be over the moon because we've never had that much exposure before.'

He sat down on his favourite bit of the bench again.

'She said it's time for us to step into the spotlight. She used the word "celebrate". I hate it when they say that, it makes me think of her *dancing*. She had things to say about the Irish, too, but they weren't very nice. I'm not going to repeat them here.'

The graffiti unicorn. How I always could pipe up with friends so much cooler than me after a large cup of the stuff. That, but not this. This was NOT IT. Fika.

Ingrid looked very un-upset. Maybe she'd seen too many people try and build careers on top of other people, and succeed at it, or she just hadn't decided which was worse yet — the massacre-romance or the modern Scandi hype. We should talk about IKEA sometime.

'Tarbuck's daughter,' Algot said. 'She works in one of the Swedish cafes, the one with the T-shirts that say "How about a fika?" She has brunch there on the weekends, says it's friendly and delicious. She says she had the idea last week when she was sinking her teeth into a cinnamon bun.'

'No one has a cinnamon bun for brunch,' I said.

Algot went over to his sword and shield, which he'd thrown on the floor when he first came in from the Parade. He put them away behind a sack of grain, making sure there was plenty of barley in front to hide them. Then Phyllis, the admin assistant, came down to take a picture, which meant that he had to dig it all out again. This is done every year after the Parade. The image gets framed and hung up in the office corridor, one in a line of winners for people to look at in the toilet queue.

Before going home, I went to see Joanne Tarbuck. This was after hours, when it was fine for her to speak to me in English again. The whole office smelt of posh coffee. Don't think the worst, I thought, there is a childhood here somewhere. It needn't always be people rubbing something in or pointing something out. Still, I stood in the doorway and didn't move until she'd offered me some. No wandering mother today either. I told her that I'd had an idea about Solveig which would both renew and enliven the Norse exhibition, something which none of the others had yet. The latter, I knew, would make her face melt.

'A pregnant Viking!' she yelled.

Her joy was even more, just more, than I'd thought. She had to take a couple of breaths.

'Our staff does consist mainly of students and the elderly,' she said, grabbing on to her desk. 'But I have thought of this for some time. You just need to be careful with these things. If I'm completely honest, I would have thought you were too feminist for the fat suit.'

'Should we maybe call it something else?' I said.

'Maybe something will come to us,' she said.

She asked me if I wanted a mint.

'I'm still drinking this delicious coffee,' I said.

'Interesting,' she said. 'I never thought you'd be in the job for the long haul. If you don't take a genuine pride in your home culture, as well as in providing the best possible experience and customer service of course, you shouldn't be in this job. That's my take on it anyway.'

'Now,' I said.

'What?'

'Now I'd like the mint, please.'

She had not asked me to sit down, but I had. I couldn't stop thinking about this now.

'There's not much to it, really, is there?' she said. 'They've just reprinted those bloody brochures, but that's fine. I have favours to cash in. We could just add a line to the East Bu page to highlight your new condition and maybe something about the cultural traditions concerning pregnancy in Viking Scotland etc, etc. Ooooh we could introduce a ritual! A ritual would be the perfect thing.'

Ingrid is going to lose her sheet over this.

'As for budget, I should have it covered but I'll need to do some research.'

'Budget?' I said. 'What are you buying?'

'The fat suit!' said Joanne Tarbuck. 'I bet the good ones are pricey. We need to get you one that doesn't look like you're carrying around a balloon under your costume.'

101

In Swedish it's a

    låtsasmage.   pretend belly.

I won't know what it looks like until Wednesday, as it will take a few days for it to arrive.

Joanne Tarbuck tentatively touched her upper lip with her middle finger, on which she wore a ring so thin it seemed unnecessary. I hoped someone had given that to her and that she hated it. There was an erupted spot on her upper lip. If she hadn't brought her hand to her face, I wouldn't have noticed it and wouldn't have to try not to stare at it.

'Management have been talking to me about innovation in the team for months,' she said. 'It will make it much more lifelike. They would have had kids, for sure. They would have spawned like it was nobody's business.'

She held up her coffee mug in front of her face. It said 'I'd rather be making music!'

'Is it true?' I said.

'What?'

Above it her eyes were large and darker than expected, a bit like tunnels.

'So, you haven't been put off by the protests?' she said.

There was another one last week. They're only small, but they're loud and every time they bring more flags, an improvised mix of Union Jacks and, perversely, St George.

'Wee bampots,' Joanne Tarbuck said.

'I tend to walk around them,' I said. 'I generally put on my sunglasses and just go for it.'

She was making a mental note now, I could tell.

102

'I thought you were getting tired of Solveig. Our last wife only lasted two years.'

This was news to me. The way people talk about the last Solveig, they make it sound like she was here since the beginning. If this is true, it means that I've already outgrown her. I'm entire heads past her.

'Not at all,' I said. 'I love working here. This is about future-proofing.'

I looked out through her window at a good portion of the place which was her home, which I do love. I could only just make out the shoulders of Fife.

'Have you finished?' she said.

She'd been sucking on her mint and sipping on the coffee at the same time, as if taste buds were beneath her. I thanked her for seeing me.

'You're so small,' she said, seeing me out.

'I'm so excited,' I said.

About that hip flask, Bobe, as I feel we need to mention it before you start getting ideas about fixing another potential problem. I only started bringing it with me when I went up to full-time after graduation and it all got a bit too early, too little sleep. I mean, I could feel the cow dung on myself in the night and dreamt of elephants. It was more about knowing it was there and I never really drink any. Sometimes I hold it and sniff it in Translation Room, but I've had maybe two sips from it in two years. In terms of now, and of Project, I genuinely haven't had any since it started. This, now, is indeed something a Pregnant Person would do, is it not?

Every night seems to need less sleep, and the days less awakeness? Hence all

chronicling   kroniserande

to make something chronic, as in a condition, forever?

If you're making up a word in one language, why not throw in two at once, double your chances. At my last count there were nineteen Post-it notes: BOKHYLLA, RAM, GARDINER, EKORRE, SPINDEL, TUMME, SÄNG, LAMPA, SÄNGLAMPA, (since you discovered the logic of 'breast warts' you've been actively seeking out compound nouns), BYRÅ, KYLSKÅP, KAFFEBRYGGARE, STOL, KÖKSMATTA (I've stepped on it so many ficking times now and every time you come after me, like a smartly dressed elf in Lego-slippers, to put it back on the rug because, why? *What could actually happen?*), BADRUM, TOALETTSTOL, TVÅL, BADKAR. The list follows a trajectory, from the bedroom to the lounge and to the kitchen corner, then to the bathroom. At this point, it's the room less labelled. A pair of your discoloured boxer shorts hangs over the towel rack, petrified with historical value: KALSONGER.

Another email you wrote back then:

> During freshers' week a girl asked me about my first
> memory of coffee. I think she was nervous and high,
> so she was asking everyone she met the same thing
> and had landed on this, poor thing. I told her I was

given only black coffee at my Brazilian orphanage, and she told me I was being a wanker, that she'd actually volunteered at an orphanage in the summer and I shouldn't assume. I walked off. What the feck did I want, applause?

In May, two years ago, when I was back in Umeå for a week and you were here, you wrote:

> Mr Strachan makes me laugh. He looks so young. He also says he doesn't like his family and that he sometimes goes to the job centre because that's where the craic is. The only bit of him that's sagging is the skin under his eyes. It looks a bit like lava. He's really ninety-seven and has leukaemia but you'd never tell. Must be hard to look so many miles away from the way things are inside. Crumbling, like. He's obsessed with shopping channels but never buys anything. The other day he told me that the term 'troubled times' is taking the piss. He says the papers overuse it and that's why he doesn't read them. He's certainly not more troubled now than he was in the eighties. I asked him if he ever worried about flying in the eighties, or about refugee camps and the alt-right. 'I've flown once in my life and it was to my daughter's wedding,' he told me. 'My ex-wife paid for it for the sake of appearances.' Mr Strachan has not once asked me where I'm from. I didn't ask him how he voted in any of the referendums.

Oh, golly it is, isn't it, this wee hovel is the safest place in the world? Turn off all the screens, close the curtains, and it may take some time before we are found by the wrong people, before we become the wrong people, or before we need help, before the future comes.

I look up the damn word. I think I need a third or fourth opinion. The word 'fika', by the way, comes from the word 'kaffi' tossed around, which apparently meant 'coffee' in nineteenth-century Sweden. During high school we would meet for a fika and have nothing but tea — but we still called it a 'fika'. Not this. Definitely not this, anyway.

This evening, you'd got hold of a couple of copies of *Dagens Nyheter* from about two weeks ago. I was about to ask you how, and how much it had cost us, but instead I sat down to look through the culture section. It had been a long day. I don't always have the energy to repeat things as many times as it takes for us to get anywhere.

I said:

| 'Du skulle ju spara ihop | 'You were meant to be saving |
| till nya glasögon.' | for new glasses.' |

You very well un-understood.

| 'Nej, tack,' | 'No, thank you,' |

you said.

My dad always told me off for fishing out the culture section of the newspaper when I was a teenager and ignoring the rest. He called that kind of behaviour

| eskapismens vagga. | the cradle of escapism. |

'First the war in Iraq,' he said, 'then interviews with porn stars.'

I've never found an interview with a porn star in the culture section of *Dagens Nyheter* but they must be there. I haven't held a physical newspaper in my hands in a long time, either. The ink was a real novelty, seductively thick. You'd made circles with a red marker around a number of different TV programmes, including several early-2000s American crime dramas, and now you were away in the bedroom, doing push-ups. I said:

'Du vet att du inte kan titta på dem här utanför Sverige, eller hur!'	'You know you can't watch these outside of Sweden, right?'

You had also circled an episode of *Extreme Couponing*.

About ten minutes later you shouted:

'Nej! Men viktigt!'	'No! But important!'

'Oh,' I said. 'Important. That word.'

You began to sing along to Swedish radio, which made me feel cold and underage again. I closed the bedroom door and took a picture of the page you'd been marking. We could be chaining ourselves to the buildings where evil lives right now, where they're getting away with it, or at least we could be talking to people who do.

Your arse walked past me when I was sitting on the couch and you said:

'Kristin tar droooger!'	'Kristin is on druuuugs!'

You meant the *Encyclopaedia of Poisonous Plants* which I have been reading in the last few days. I seem to have come down with an addiction to short entries during these days of longitude.

I took a bath while you were on an online call with Hector, the nineteen-year-old plumber in Göteborg. He was telling you about his experience of hearing aids. I ended up falling asleep in the bath and didn't notice when the call was over, then I woke up to a knock on the door. An A5 piece of paper slowly slid underneath it and onto the tiles.

'Här!' you said through the crack and there was a scratching, the sound of feeding tarantulas.

'Till dig!'   'For you!'

I got excited. I thought maybe the old letters had returned, proper, meandering ones, full of animals. I hurried to dry off. The thing was a folded-up brochure, bellowing with the most Swedish of colours. On the cover, a chubby Swedish flag with bulging eyes, arms and legs like popsicle sticks, smiled with its mouth too open.

'Kommer du ihåg hur   'Do you remember how to
man säger att "låtsas"?'   say "to pretend"?'
said the speech bubble attached to it.

The brochure was so glossy I couldn't even crease it. It was for something called:

Stockholmsyndromet: Stockholm Syndrome:
ett förbund för svenskt   a society for Swedish
språkbevarande   language preservation

'Bobe!' I said, 'Listen up and look at me.'

I tried to push the brochure back out through the crack, but you had blocked the gap with a draft excluder. There was something stuck on the door, in the grain of the wood, which may have been old matter from one of our noses. Inside the brochure there was a picture of a bunch of mostly blonde people posing behind a white-clothed table. The table was over-blooming with food and clearly prepared for a midsummer feast. Behind all that a large tree was poking at the smiling people's heads with its branches. They looked very, very happy to be there, to be representing a sunny, super-fertile North.

'Oh, brilliant,' I said, 'they threw in some brown people to be on the safe side.'

You laughed and then you caught yourself.

'So what?' I said.

'Läs tack!'

'Read please!'

you said.

'Inte? Du är inte ensam. Många, speciellt unga människor, minns inte längre hur man säger "att låtsas". Istället använder de det svengelska uttrycket "att fejka". Så passande! Eftersom de faktiskt låtsas att det inte är svenska vi pratar i Sverige. Ju fler sådana uttryck vi använder, desto mer glömmer vi, desto mer försvagas svenskan som språk och desto svagare blir vår kultur.'

'No? You're not alone. Many, especially young people, no longer remember how to say "pretend". Instead, they use the Swenglish expression "fejking". How appropriate! Since they're actually pretending that it's not Swedish we speak in Sweden. The more expressions like this we use, the more we forget, the more the Swedish language is weakened and the weaker our culture becomes.'

'You know what this is?' I said. 'Jesus ficking Christ.'

You let out the most condescending sigh. There was some shuffling and scratching. I imagined your left foot and where it was. This was followed by another wee note slipped underneath the door, but this time you gave it a swing which jettisoned it half-way across the bathroom floor.

'INTE RASISTER!'   'NOT RACISTS!'

it said in your own capitals. Any other day you'd be suspicious of exclamation marks, because 'who's that fuckin' sure of anything?'

'Oh come on,' I said. 'I'll let you tell me off when it comes to Mrs Pullingham or any of your other fossils, but Swedish closet racists—'

'Nej! Inte,' you said.

'My aunt Cilla's village has more Swedish flags than it has people under twenty-five.'

'Read the thing, K!'

I read.

>*Stockholm Syndrome: basic principles (my translation)*
>
> The Swedish language is in danger and under threat from the hegemony of the English language in Swedish society.
>
> The preservation of the Swedish language is synonymous with the preservation of Swedish national identity.

> This preservation demands a conscious struggle for
> Swedish, against English, in the media and in science.

> This struggle should focus on the future: the child.

Ficking hell. What child? There is technically no child. And there it is:

barnet   the child

as if ONE MASSIVE CHILD was parachuting down on the whole of Sweden, obese and over-charged with sugar.

I started laughing and then I closed the thing and made myself look at the flag with the fleshy lips again to stop laughing. I couldn't see what any of this was doing to you. It was like telling a dead phone that you love it.

'Weren't you the one who said you'd never join anything with an acronym?'

Silence, a bit more scribbling, and a bird on the windowsill. Maybe *I* was the one looking in on *it*.

'Is it really easier this way, though?' I said and pushed back yet another note. 'Also, you should have called your mother yesterday. She's dreaming about your biological parents.'

Still more scribbling. You might have realised that it's the moment in your face when you're gearing up to say something, which you'll inevitably not be able to say, that's hardest to stomach.

'Du är inte intresserad,'   'You are not interested,'

the latest one said.

'Du inte förstår'   'You not understand.'

The other notes were spread around my bare knees on the bathroom tiles.

'You should see the absolute mess in here,' I said.

I didn't hear you when you got up on your side of the door, could have been when I was making small airplanes out of your notes and throwing one of them out the window down over Tall Azif's garden. Eventually it got cold.

'Start bringing your clothes into the bathroom with you,' I said.

Yes, to myself.

Because you never know when you might not have it in you to get out there again straight away.

You were back at it with another Disney already, starting and stopping to make sure of something every five minutes, and your neck was making industrial sounds.

'Vårtsvinsbarn	'Warthog child
Vårtsvinsbarn'	Warthog child,'

you professed.

You have taken to dressing for the lessons. No sweatpants, but a nice, dotted shirt and jumper which makes you look approachable to people I wouldn't want to approach myself. Only the Lego-slippers are left.

'You used to be funny,' I said, on my way to the bedroom, with nothing but the remaining paper airplanes on me.

I looked up the language society thing. According to their website, they chose the name to 'reclaim the term Stockholm Syndrome from Anglophone popular culture'. It then goes on to list how many American films, songs, and books have taken the name

Stockholm Syndrome, which to me seems not just a little counter-productive. Wasn't this supposed to be about healthy alternatives? Isn't that like saying sugar is bad and then offering nothing but an inventory of all the high-sugar content products in existence?

Before Lady Gaga and Björn Skifs, the only cow I'd ever seen up close lived in my aunt Cilla's little grey village in Skåne. Her name was Panda and she belonged to Cilla's neighbour, who was a farmer and once appeared on a reality TV show. They kept saying the cow liked me, that she was never this calm with any of the other kids. I kept stroking her, my fingers perplexed across her back, and above us other people's expectations about the nature of animals and children, until the cow got fed up and head-butted me. The other thing I remember about the small grey village is the flags: so many Swedish flags that they almost touched each other's corners, waiting for some wind to whip it all open. Last time I saw her, my aunt Cilla was hollering at my Dad across a Christmas table, about how Italy, where she now lives, has become a massive 'arrival terminal'.

'They're *all* coming!' she said.

My parents tried to say, without saying it, that Cilla's much too fragile for politics. At least she's happier now than she used to be. She puts on make-up and enters triathlons. She doesn't finish them but she *enters* them, they said, and entering makes all the difference once you're in your fifties.

språkbad   language bath
What if the words and their baggage did float around

113

like chemicals in a solution, and when you got in and stayed there long enough, they'd seep in through the pores? Before the bath, they (who are they, again?) would ask you to think about Iceland. You'd give them a few things: small horses; a bearded, grinning grandfather at the foot of a glacier; a jumper. You would now be immersed. Sometime later you'd be out of the bath and *woosh*: no more horses. Instead there would be a million complications you couldn't hand back to them, whoever they are.

In the case of the jars, the formaldehyde replaces guts and blood. It is not an adding-to but an instead-of, you explained once. I quickly get out of bed and grab Squirrel McCamp from his mantelpiece-seat. I apologise profusely to him on the bedroom floor, for everything we emptied him of. Which is when I notice you're not there. When I went to bed you were watching a documentary about the fifteenth century, when Sweden was a European super-power and people supposedly shivered at the thought of it, us.

If you weren't doing this thing, I would have told you about the Swedish king, Karl XI, who wanted to train a cavalry of moose. It didn't fail because you can't ride a moose, they just won't walk in formation. Now, you sit there with what you're missing out on.

I get up and stay behind the half-closed bedroom door. Look, Bobe, a homeseeking!

hemsöka (haunting)   homeseeking

114

Your face is there, drained by the laptop light, your cheekbones liquefied. You're digging a trench into your lower lip, munching a big, bad hole no one asked for. As I open the door less than an inch wider, the images from the laptop screen come on in. You're watching the news again. First there's an item about Syria, then about the methane in the Siberian tundra, then about gangs of ageless children in São Paulo and the drugs they use. Everyone is on silent and Tall Azif is awake downstairs, sneezing.

'Hey, Bobe, that's the hellhole where you're from!'

I would never even think of saying, but I do think: where did you come from? And it's true that I don't get it. Your eyes, hands, tongue, thighs are all busy deciphering the Swedish subtitles instead of looking at the urgencies, one after the other, past whatever story they were trying to tell. You keep chewing throughout. When they speak too quickly for you to keep up, you groan and stop the video, stare at it, start again.

I've never asked you if you've ever wanted to find your birth parents. I know you'd say no but I've never asked. Meanwhile I'm desperately needing to wee.

pissnödig   pissneedy

I do adore Swedish sometimes (as long as it stays where it is). The way it pulls the parts it needs together and makes do is so practical. 'Swedish', as an ad for a hardware company says: 'functional'.

I'm really ficking pissneedy now, but I'm not getting out and walking past you in that state. That is not happening. The dirty plates on the lounge table look infectious. Growing up, my mum used to repeat at least once a day that leaving dirty dishes on the floor is the first sign that someone no longer likes themselves very much. There are crumbs on the floor so small they must be ancient, trodden down to fractions underneath our feet. We missed this when it happened, and now we're waltzing across it with the crap sticking to our skin, waiting for the other person to grab the hoover. This is what they call a fundamental problem, a human problem.

'What are you the most scared of?'

I definitely don't say either.

You don't look over to my side and I stay exactly where I am.

When a minute has passed and you still aren't looking, what happens is fairly easy to predict. What happens is this: I begin to visualise a tiny needle emptying my bladder slowly and so effectively, like a measure implemented by a governing body. At this point you do move, but only to crawl up to the laptop and move the cursor to the beginning of the video, play it again: the faces, the emergencies, again. You make notes slowly and meticulously, one frame at a time. I piss myself all in one go.

My mother was thirty-seven when she had me. That's thirteen years from whatever it is that's going on here, an entire new teenager with gross mood swings and the start of a stubble. Twenty-four is very much not too young and not too old to have a kid. It's so bang-in-the-middle of my fertility window, in fact, that I'm enveloped by every extreme — I am the safest meridian. What does that matter when there's something stuck in the throat of the future and it won't budge?

If I were my own mother: I'd have had thirteen more years to think about the Future before it arrived full of holes.

If the Future came now: we'd be in separate rooms and you would have fallen asleep, drooling across the keyboard, a small gut flap over your waistband. You'd stay a half-baked nurse and I'd never find out why it's called 'custard'.

Not everyone was a zombie during the world wars,

you wrote on some run-of-the-mill Tuesday,

but if it was between me and someone else, I'm seriously fucking terrified that I wouldn't choose them.

If the Future happened today: I'd have no idea how to say hello.

Tuesday

I fell asleep only once I didn't feel like sleeping anymore, then it was six am and you were cocooned where my toes used to be. I touched your nose with one of them, but you did not wake up.

'I dub thee,' I said, and you turned to your left side, then I ran out of ideas.

I got up and went to work via the washing machine. Last time I weed myself I was six and busy catching tadpoles on the edge of a swamp. It was a good environment for an accident.

'Still a night owl,' your ma said when I told her you were still asleep. 'Tell him to call me but not before six tonight because I'll be in class. This woman is amazing. Such tendons!'

She was most likely talking about one of the instructors at her yoga retreat, but it could also have been the bus driver. It's difficult to tell whose legs your mum is paying attention to at any particular time. I put the phone down and was annoyed with her for not noticing that nothing is safe anymore.

I asked for more loo roll from Hugh in maintenance and he looked at me as if thinking that we shit too much, the Norse. We should be shitting exactly the same amount as all the other Peoples. Algot has a minor gut condition that makes him go to

119

the loo more often than the rest of us, but not enough for Hugh to make it any of his business.

Joanne Tarbuck winked at me when she hurried past the storage hut. The belly is meant to arrive tomorrow. It will be a silicone, thirty-five-week belly with boobs and I'm supposed to go to Joanne Tarbuck's office in the morning for a fitting session. I'd have thought it's as simple as strapping it on and off you go, but knowing Joanne Tarbuck she will have gone for something fancy, something requiring steps. I have a hairy back — I can't have things taped on to me.

I only really miss you when I go back to your old letters, because you haven't gone anywhere. When I miss you is when I can't help picking at the letters. You're going back to work on Thursday. I said I'd call the GP on Wednesday. I could become properly pregnant shortly after that. If I got pregnant on Wednesday, I'd be pregnant by the time the festivals kick off. I'd be one of the pregnant ones and you'd go back to work living with a pregnant person. Perhaps you would ask me things about my bowel movements.

This afternoon, we burned Einar again. Poppy from costume design makes them in multiples out of straw, about once a month. She dresses all the Einars in discarded bits from old uniforms, and she's pretty indiscriminate about it, to the point where sometimes Einar wears long eighteenth-century dresses. Sometimes he has what looks like glitter around his waist which blinks and catches in the flames, but luckily the public aren't allowed to get close enough to notice. Einar himself is someone beyond all of this — a face and a way of walking which we all remember. Without him, we wouldn't have come to Scotland in the first place. Solveig, Ingrid, Algot, all of us, have memories of him once killing a man and giving his corpse to the wolves. We know that he used to drive his family out of the dwelling-house on summer nights with his snoring. He picked up his children from their cradles to show them the moon.

'Look at those arms,' he used to say of every single baby.

Either he had a serious ambition, or something at home scared him enough to pack up his stuff, his family, and run all the way out of Scandinavia.

Ingrid and I take turns lighting the fire on Crown Square. She's supposed to be Einar's widow and the spiritual leader of the family so we're guessing that someplace, at some point, the honour did befall her, but she also has a bad shoulder. Over time we've come to agree on a choreography. First, we both walk up to the pyre and stand in front of it, eyes down, for as long as it takes for people to be quiet. A few times I've seen Ingrid check her watch. She'll tell anyone else off for wearing one. It's always unexpected when someone wants to get away as much or as often as you do. Once the crowd is silent, we make the torch nod at the pile of branches, paper, and cardboard.

'Núna!'   'Now!'

Ingrid whispers.

Once the fire is lit, we usually retreat with our backs to the audience, because it seems disrespectful to turn your back on your burning father-in-law/husband, but last week there was an incident. A tourist tried to take a selfie and singed his hair, so we had to cordon off the pyre. As a result, today Ingrid and I had to get over the tape after lighting the fire. I half-jumped over it and Ingrid went underneath. My foot got tangled in it; I lost my balance and fell. Looking up, both palms full of small bits of gravel, I saw the first belly. It was right there, ready to receive me like an air bag, had I been backing away from the fire. The girl's smile was hot and setting like a sun over it.

'What the fick!' I said, in the wrong language, before Ingrid grabbed me and hauled me to the back of the crowd.

From behind the girl, it was impossible to even see the outlines of the belly. She was holding it up with a straight back, arms innocently at either side. It wasn't changing the rest of her in the slightest.

'Is ------ ---------?' Ingrid whispered, digging into my arm with her thumb.

'Of course not!' I hissed. 'She wasn't pregnant yesterday, was she? She was just Irish Karen.'

'That's private,' Algot said sternly. 'Perhaps she was and perhaps she wasn't.'

Ingrid made her neck crackle. There were other bellies, too. One was standing in the corner between the Great Hall and the Royal Palace, the girl looking straight at me. Another two were walking past at the edges, showing off from every angle, their faces glistening. The fake bellies must be making them sweat more than their usual corsets. Even the aristocracy wanted in on this.

'Five,' I said.

'Seven,' Algot corrected. 'I reckon that means something for these people? Why seven?'

I wanted to spit on something that wouldn't mind it so much. Ingrid patted me on the arm and offered me the flagon which I pushed away.

'Ladies,' Algot whispered.

People were beginning to doubt the quality of our heartbreaks. I leant in toward Ingrid:

'Falskur magi,' I said.

'Já,' said Ingrid, and smoothened the front of my petticoat.

'What? What is she saying?'

'It's all going on without us,' Algot said, looking over at a devastated group of tourists.

'Can you please tell me what she just said?'

Having never been that close to Ingrid's ear before, I was surprised at how it wasn't nearly as wrinkled as the rest of her face. She held her hand over her chest and nodded.

'Diego,' she said.

'Who's that?' I said.

'She says she may have told Diego about your pregnancy,' Algot said. 'Solveig's pregnancy. He works in the box office. They do bell-ringing together on the weekends.'

'You!' I said and I think I even poked Ingrid's shoe a little with my shoe.

She rolled her eyes and crossed her chest. Sometimes we make them both converted Christians, for the added conflict. You think someone is one of the good ones and then they roll their eyes at you, and it feels like they've dropped you from the third floor, with no intention to wait and check how you land.

'Joanne Tarbuck incoming,' Algot said. 'She's wearing the heels.'

'Why would you do that?' I said.

'I read somewhere that they never really existed, Vikings,' someone said, walking past. 'It's a Hollywood thing.'

When Joanne Tarbuck wears the heels it usually means she wasn't planning to pay us a visit. Her dress suit looked particularly out of place in the light of living flames. She could just as well have roared in on a motorcycle. Having stomped across the square, she placed a hand on my arm, then lifted it again and pointed to her watch. She held up six fingers and pointed up to the Royal Palace, then she marched back, past the nearest belly, with her elbows out.

'She wants you to come and see her as soon as you finish,' Algot explained.

'Thanks,' I said. 'I got that.'

'At six o'clock,' said Algot.

'I feel like learning something interesting today,' another tourist said, someone who was clearly heading for the exit.

We finished the ritual ticking every box but one: sometimes Ingrid sings during the burning, but she didn't do that today. She told Algot that she felt bad about having mentioned Solveig's pregnancy plans and sad that I thought it might have been deliberate. It's even possible that she apologised, but Algot had just gone to get a shovel, so he wasn't there to translate that part. There may be an apology out there, evaporating between the two of us like the booze.

After every fire, the four of us (three this time, as Sigurd was away) are responsible for the clean-up. The surrounding buildings prevent most of the smoke from spreading beyond Crown Square, but they also help create a soggy ash-cloud between them. We gave it the name 'Yggdrasil', after the universal tree, which is the only thing we've ever named together, the four of us. Last summer, the people working in the offices around the square tried to get the Einar burnings moved to East Bu itself, but failed because of the risk of revenue loss. The fire, at the heart of the Castle, is one of the most popular events on the regular schedule. People have been known to plan their entire visits to coincide with it. They come just to see Einar burn.

Two men came over to me when I was shovelling ashes into a wheelbarrow. They both had very small hands and one of them seemed to be naturally bald. The other one, I thought, might have shaved his head just to keep him company. They stayed so close to each other, holding up each other's pace, but it didn't seem to keep either of them from moving. I kept on shovelling as they looked on. When it happens automatically, which is more and more often, not-understanding is like scrolling past a story that just doesn't fit into your day, no matter who's telling it: a habitual, easier and easier un-seeing which escapes with you.

'She doesn't speak English, Patrick,' said one of the men.

He had a strange way of holding his partner's hand, hovering around every single finger but not properly touching any of them.

'Doesn't she?' said Patrick. 'Don't you, darling? I thought you had to, to work in this country.'

'Sverigedemokraterna är Sveriges tredje största parti,' I said.

'The Swedish Democrats are Sweden's third-largest party,'

'Sorry?' said Patrick.

'De startades av nynazister.' 'They were founded by neo-Nazis.'

'Did you say something about a party?' Patrick said.

'Va?' 'What?' I said.

Patrick smelt like strawberries.

'It's not right,' said the first guy. 'I bet they all have asthma. I'd wager it goes against regulations.'

'Can we help, darling?' said Patrick.

He ended up losing a ring among the debris while helping me shovel. It wasn't his wedding ring, he said, so it was okay. He said this three times throughout the forty-five minutes we spent looking.

'Jag är ledsen,' 'I am sad and sorry,'

I said, and it felt good to be able to say both, and at the same time.

'This used to be such a beautiful place,' said Patrick's husband.

Instead of the ring, we found a hand in the ashes. Poppy must have used a mannequin for part of this particular Einar. Patrick's husband was in stitches about it.

'What an adventure,' he said. 'I bet your sister would be all over this any day, Pat.'

It's nine thirty pm in the Translation Room and the cleaners haven't arrived yet. Someone did say that they cheat. It's even possible that I and the cows are the only ones left on site. That's immense, just in case anything should happen — to consider just what it would take for me to go outside and *see* to it.

There shouldn't be any corners in the clock tower (it's round) but people have stuffed so many things in here that we've created nooks and divisions, a room out of a tunnel. There are boxes, the cupboard with the tea things, a first-aid kit, and some kind of ball, possibly Pilates, rolling from one side to the other when there's the slightest draught. In the film, they're already at sea. A really brilliant bit coming up now: when Sigurd hacks into an old and decrepit enemy (someone's lover, I think, but that gets explained in the sections I don't have) with an axe and the blood erupts straight out of a garden hose.

I've never watched the film in the evening before.

You sent me a message with the link to that Stockholm-Syndrome-thing website. There's an article on there about how English-language TV shows have completely overtaken Swedish programming in the last few decades. This explains all the highlighted programmes in the paper yesterday. The group is especially upset about a French documentary on the resistance during WWII. Allegedly, it was first dubbed into English before it was given Swedish subtitles and aired on Swedish TV. Your message itself said only:

127

'Titta'   'Look'

As if I was in the habit of closing my eyes when opening text messages.

I notice that the group — the cult more like — shorten their name to StS. Now that's a relief. There's another article about how most Swedish universities are now demanding that their postgraduate students write their dissertations in English. It argues that Swedish as a language of science is almost dead. Extinct. Screwed. They make an effort to use many imported words in order to illustrate their point.

A question for you: in the great range of Great Dangers, how high do you think an endangered language ranks, especially if it's not really endangered, only its ego?

Then there is another text:

'onsdag,' it says.

'Onsdag imorgon.'   'Wednesday morning.'

'Yes, indeed,' I reply. 'Wednesday follows upon Tuesday and so until the end of days.'

'Du sa onsdag för ring,   'You said Wednesday for
ring, bara du slår doktor   ring, ring, why don't you
signal.'   give doctor a call.'

'I'm not coming home if you ever quote Abba again.'

A pause, during which I hear your cough transplanted across the sound of a woodpecker.

'You worry about injustice,' I write. 'Water shortage. That's what you worry about.'

'Oro,' you write. 'O-ro!'

Now that is, actually, quite cool.

'I know exactly what you mean,' I write.

I turn my phone off because who wants to constantly be reminded of the way things used to be?

worry	oro
ro	tranquillity
oro	un-tranquillity

That is what this thing is — an un-tranquilliser.

This afternoon, I noticed that someone has given Joanne Tarbuck a new mug. This one has flying nuns on it but no clues about where they are planning to go. She'd moved her desk to the middle of the room, which meant she was now able to walk around it in circle after circle as she spoke, but it didn't leave much space for visitors. I had to stand back against the wall. My left foot smelt heavily of Solveig. I'd buried it deep in ash and cindered twigs. Where are all those bellies now? Have they been discarded or taken for runs?

'They ordered them all from Amazon Prime,' said Joanne Tarbuck. 'Amateurs. They look like shite, too. Haven't they got the slightest eye for quality, these folks? I bet you they're all foam. Didn't those bellies look cheap to you?'

'Sub,' I said. 'Substandard. Yeah, from where I was standing maybe a bit.'

What I was thinking was that Solveig wouldn't know what foam was unless it was at sea.

'Where is mine coming from then?' I asked.

129

'I've ordered it from an independent manufacturer, family-owned, decent company in Glasgow. Silicone all the way through which apparently yields better to the touch. Obviously, it was going to take at least a day to get something good, but those Lithuanians couldn't wait.'

'Tricky,' I said.

'Lithuanians,' she said. 'Who did you tell?'

'Woah,' I said.

'I didn't,' I said.

This could have been true. I stayed quiet for Joanne Tarbuck to make up her mind about it.

'Lithuanians,' she said again.

I was reminded that for a few months, about a year ago, she'd had an assistant and her name was Amy. What happened to her? She was never talked about anymore.

'Are we still? You know?' I said.

'Are we going ahead with it? You bet we are, pet. I'll come and see you when it arrives tomorrow, and we'll talk. For now, I need to think. The numpties, I swear it was Daniel. He's been after an edge for his People for years. Now he thinks they'll have the limelight. There's nothing special about the Lithuanians and he knows it. He's perfectly aware, you know, their days are numbered. They hardly left anything behind, did they? You tell me where you've seen a Lithuanian street name.'

'Nowhere that I can think of,' I said.

'Keep thinking and you still won't,' she said. 'It's not a popular thing to say out there, but you have to leave something behind to be remembered. To matter. That's exactly what we try to encourage with the Parade. Some healthy competition. Think about how you'll be remembered. How you've been of use. Now with the talk of Bangladeshis and Syrians wanting in. The more people want in, the more useful you need to be. That's not being racist is it? It's just history.'

I looked outside, through Joanne Tarbuck's window which was so much *her* window, infused with Joanne Tarbuckness all over because of the curtains, her accent, the way I was balancing on my sit bones whenever she got excited, thinking I might have to leave, and I had this feeling that the entire Castle would one day be under attack again, but not a historical one. It was impossible to decide what might mean something then, the street names or whatever: the cake.

'I've been looking into Viking birth ceremonies,' she said. 'And there's so very much of interest. Not all of it will be to Ingrid's liking, but she'll live.'

Would she, though? I was still looking out the window. The buildings falling, the random shot of stone to ground through someone's head. Ingrid had a bad knee and might not make it.

'I just don't understand how he heard about it so quickly,' Joanne Tarbuck continued. 'He probably saw the order confirmation in my email inbox. I may have to launch an enquiry.'

'Were all the bellies Lithuanian?' I said.

I couldn't stop looking out through the window. That section of the city, right there, will go under water first.

'They have friends everywhere,' she said. 'They find it very easy to live like that.'

131

When she opened the door to let me out, I thought: I might as well ask, in this day and age.

'Have you ever worn one?'

'A what?' she said, staring at the watering can she'd just grabbed.

'One of those bellies. Have you ever tried one on?'

'Ha,' she said and stood very still, like she was waiting for a hiccup.

'Only the real thing, pet,' she said then. 'But that's for another day.'

With that, she began ushering me out. I wanted to see what she'd do after I'd left, to ask her when, how? To ask her to tell me about the time before it's too late, about trusting the receiving end of your child, but by the time I'd formulated the beginning of a question, I was already out. Someone in the direction of the barracks had smuggled in an illicit musical instrument and she was about to open the window to put an end to that.

If I were Solveig: I bet there was a thing I used every day of my life, which was not the thing I thought would disappear first. So many languages and their unfolding through every little thing.

Don't think I haven't noticed how you have the å almost under control, at least when it comes before a single consonant, as in the word for Pope. The ö and the ä are still flapping in their own merry way. Beer turns into an eel. The worst part is when you're visibly convinced you have a whole sentence ready to

132

deliver. I can see it coming. You spit it out and I have to come running after it to work out its nature. Most of the time I can see what you're trying to say but only through a very filthy window.

'Vad aaaaar "cool" på   'What is "cool" in
svenska?'   Swedish?'

you say.

'"Cool",' I said. 'Sometimes "coolt", depending on the noun.'

'Cool? As in, just "cool"?' you said.

'You see they have a point, right?' you said. 'English has taken over.'

The term Stockholm Syndrome wasn't the term Stockholm Syndrome at all when it was born. On 23 August 1973, a man called Jan-Erik Olsson went into a branch of Kreditbanken at Norrmalmstorg in central Stockholm and demanded three million SEK. He also wanted a convicted bank robber, Clark Olofsson, to be brought over from prison. Four hostages, a bizarre call to the prime minister, a few explosions, and six days later, both men were arrested and the hostages taken to safety. One of them was Kristin Enmark, a twenty-three-year-old secretary. She was the one who asked the prime minister to please allow her to leave with the robbers. Later, she became involved in a sexual relationship with Clark Olofsson. Studying her case, a psychiatrist coined the term 'Norrmalstorgsyndromet'. Obviously, after Norrmalstorg, which was where it happened.

Norrmalmstorg   North island square

133

The following year, Patty Hearst, a rich American girl, was kidnapped and joined the guerrilla group who kidnapped her. She was publicly diagnosed with what was now referred to as Stockholm Syndrome, and it had nothing to do with Stockholm anymore.

Something else: every time I say the word 'translated' I say it differently, like I'm standing on one of those Saturn-shaped exercise balls, practising my balance. Don't look at me.

I also noticed that you did a bit of preservation work in the bathroom yesterday, even though it wasn't specifically on the schedule. It's the brand-new mouse. What kind of person stands and sniffs the remains of formaldehyde in the air to comfort themselves? It's supposed to make you think of corpses. There is no evidence left of me pissing myself.

They don't turn the alarms on until after they're done cleaning the offices, so I managed to get out of the Palace without anyone noticing I'd been there after hours. I only know about the alarm routines because of the one time I spoke to Dave Boyle and he told me he often stays late ('Because this job takes over your life, love'), consuming entire packs of digestive biscuits instead of dinners. He so clearly had to say all of that. When I first started at the Castle, I was told never to look out the window when in Translation Room, because if I could see the view, then the view could see me (or the glare from my TV). It would ruin everything.

'Everything!' they said.

The stones on Crown Square looked so blue and unburdened at night. Without the weight of visitors, they could have been a checked quilt held down only by its sides. There's a narrow corridor between two buildings in one corner of the square, where lights were pushing past each other from the city centre below, never getting any closer. I worried a little about the CCTV and stuck to the sides of buildings. You have to assume a head isn't particularly recognisable without the scarf.

When I got to Argyll Battery I walked straight over to the wall and crouched down there for a bit, in case someone down on Princes Street saw me and either reported me to the police or assumed I was an exclusive party they'd want an invitation to. It's very festive down there at the moment: a simmering soup of wooohooos and fuck yeahs. The festivalgoer sounds just like the hen night which isn't too far off the smashed nose. When I first came here, I'd sometimes go down to Princes Street Gardens just to sit and look up at the Castle from below. Finished, set, was how I thought of it, so whole it dried my eyes out. The same thing happens when I look at a lake really early in the morning, the surface miles away from breaking, so complete regardless of what happens on the shore, even if there was carnage and it happened to be our fault. Then I started working inside the Castle walls, I moved in and the Castle shrank — it became dusty and broke very easily.

Sometimes I think of either of us: 'You are one of those who live here.'

If I'd said this to you any day over the past three years, over

135

any hum of our toothbrushes, you would have asked which lake, precisely, I was referring to, and why would I swim so early in the morning? Was it very hot and was this my usual routine?

'When was this, K–bite, exactly?' you would have said.

'It was at some point back there,' I'd say. 'Before.'

There were voices from over by the Lithuanian Mining Village, which is in the old Cart Shed. I dove to hide behind a cannon and landed knees first on the gravel.

'Your name, please?' someone said, not to me, thankfully.

There should be a hyphen between Mining and Village in all the museum signs, because it's not the type of mining that's specifically Lithuanian, but the village. At the end of last summer, someone brought management's attention to the Lithuanian community at Newtongrange during the early 1900s. They built a whole fake coal mine underneath Argyle Battery over the winter season. Visitors like being taken down into the dark, and they love returning to the surface for ice cream afterward. There's going to be an evaluation this autumn, pitting customer satisfaction against wages and upkeep–costs. Like Joanne Tarbuck said, when you look up and there's nothing left to touch, you wonder: were they ever really here?

'Your name, sir!' someone said again.

'I think you should let him ask at least three times before you answer,' said someone with an Eastern European accent. 'And look very confused. You know? Shake your head, maybe scratch it a bit if you want to look really daft. Which I guess maybe you do?'

'Does he?' said someone else. 'Is daft really to our advantage here?'

Someone else again told them to be quiet.

'Your name, please, sir. Now thank you!'

This was an Irish guy I recognised. In real life he's actually from Birmingham, but he's phenomenal with all kinds of accents. In front of him was one of the Lithuanians. He'd combed so much gel into his hair that you could see it glistening even in the dusk. The Irish guy pointed at himself and said:

'Me Mr Crossley. You?'

'Darius Urbansomethingsomething,' said the gelatinous guy.

For one cut-out second, I thought that maybe they had an audience somewhere that I hadn't spotted, but after scanning the whole battery it was still just us.

'Right,' said this Mr Crossley the Irish guy. 'Daryl Urban it is then.'

He was making notes. A line of other people stood shuffling behind Daryl Urban. They began to whisper to each other now, some of them laughing.

'Dudes,' said Daryl Urban. 'Fucking shut up or they'll hear us down there.'

When he said that they all took a long look down at the masses. I did, too. Someone was in fact crawling up the slope where no one should be crawling at all. There are paths for that, even during festival time.

If I were pregnant and this was long ago, perhaps I'd be in pre-birth confinement. I don't know if they did that kind of thing, perhaps that came later, in the Middle Ages. Perhaps I'd literally be behind a wall.

It was about half ten now.

'Go on then,' Daryl Urban said, 'let's run through it before security get here. I told Carmen we'd be fixing costumes till late, but it'll look weird if we're standing around too long. They'll get it on the cameras.'

'They never check the cameras.'

'Do you want them to have a reason to check the cameras?'

'You leave the cameras to me,' someone said.

'Jesus, Jo,' Daryl Urban said. 'What have you been watching?'

'You will be working in the mines,' said Mr Crossley.

Daryl Urban didn't reply. My right leg had fallen asleep, from the foot all the way up my right arse cheek, and I kept thinking that perhaps my phone wasn't on silent. I wanted another text from you. I certainly didn't want to know what you were busy with.

'What?' said Daryl. 'What do you want me to do now?'

'Man, you wrote the script!' said Mr Crossley. 'Like, I don't know, look like you don't understand a word of what I'm saying. How did you get this job if you can't do that?'

'Shall I stand with my mouth agape?' said Daryl. 'Mr Crossley? Would that suit your envisioned level of cluelessness?'

'Look at your wife for guidance,' said a very tall girl behind Daryl.

'Who's my wife?' said Daryl.

'It's twenty to eleven,' said the girl.

'The coal mines,' said Mr Crossley again. 'You will be working in the coal mines.'

Daryl turned to the line of five people behind him. He shook his head slowly. The rest of them also shook their heads and lifted their hands as if to say: I have no idea what he's talking about. I do not understand what he's saying, please help. At this point, Mr Crossley reverted to charades. He dug at the ground with an imaginary spade and threw make-believe dirt to the sides, over his shoulder, in every direction. If it were real dirt it would have grated his eyes. He wiped sweat off his forehead. He dug, he threw, he wiped again.

'Ah! Yes!' said Daryl.

'Yes!' he said, and then he added a whole stream of Lithuanian.

The other five chimed in, enthusiastically; they nodded to each other. Daryl stood to one side, and another guy took his place. That person was asked for his name, too, and Mr Crossley proceeded to give him a completely different name. The whole pattern was repeated.

'And then we're all led down into the black hole,' said Daryl.

'Now the speech,' said the wife, yawning.

'You should do it,' said Mr Crossley.

'Ha,' said Daryl. 'They won't like that.'

'They'll hate it,' said Mr Crossley. 'I'll make sure my team leader goes to get the rota at exactly ten o'clock tomorrow so that she can hear it and hate it, too, the bigoted fucker.'

'Do you actually just want to get sacked, Phil?' said Daryl's wife.

'I don't want to be one of them,' said Phil/Mr Crossley. 'The way this place is run is shite for you and it's shite for everyone.'

The girl who'd played Daryl's wife stepped up, pulled a phone out of her pocket and up to her face. She wore glasses and three nose piercings, all of that came out of the night at once. She scrolled and swiped a few times, then cleared her throat. My phone vibrated. This could be when you looked up, looked at the time, and said: 'Hey, that's late, she should have been home by now?'

'Ladies and gentlemen. The scene we have just witnessed is a re-enactment of the welcoming many Lithuanians received upon arrival in Scotland at the turn of the last century.'

She wasn't really reading. She knew it all by heart.

'A considerable number of them set out for America, and when they arrived here, they weren't told that this wasn't America.'

Some of the others laughed. The woman who was going to sabotage the CCTV said she was freezing her balls off and they laughed at this as well.

'They were farmers, and they wanted nothing more than to continue farming in a place with a bit less religious persecution and harassment. A little less danger for their lives and the lives of their children. The problem was that digging coal and ploughing a field look very similar when you're playing charades, especially if you don't have a reason to expect coal-digging to be an option in the first place. You can imagine, then, how these people were treated by their fellow miners once their new colleagues realised that the newcomers had no idea what they were doing. Through no fault of their own, by the way. That they didn't know how to say "look out!" or "turn left" or "catch you numpty".'

'You should maybe rephrase that last bit,' said Daryl. 'It's rather clunky.'

'Fuck it,' said someone else. 'Let's go down in the mines and get hammered.'

'That would be inadvisable,' said Daryl.

Daryl's wife continued:

'The Museum of Immigration favours entertainment above all else,' she said. 'They don't allow us to speak English because they say it should feel authentic, and that we should be celebrating the wealth of cultures which made Scotland what it is today. Really it means we're not able to talk to you. We can't tell our story, because telling it doesn't make them any money. We're here to announce that we're going on strike, until we're allowed to use English to answer any questions the public may have.'

'On a daily basis,' Mr Crossley added.

'On a daily basis, obviously,' she repeated and gave Mr Crossley the finger.

'Aren't you going to mention anything about there not being any Pakistani people in the museum? Pakistanis are the fourth largest non-UK-born group in Scotland, way above the Irish.'

'Jesus, Jo, one thing at a time okay?'

'And then I thank them for listening, and then we all go down into the mines.'

Someone began to laugh again, but all on their own they sounded like a baby goat.

I was only half a lower body now; my leg was so deeply asleep. There was shrieking from down Princes Street Gardens, and someone shouted: 'I love you, you cunt.'

'Obviously not that much!' Daryl's wife shouted and they all ran toward the staff exit.

I hung back for a while longer, worried about being seen, and because there had been quite a few texts from you.

'Mitt nya favoritord:	'My new favourite word:
sköldpadda.'	turtle.'
Sköld–padda	Shield-toad
'Kommer hem??'	'Coming home??'
'Vi inte är gamla.'	'We not are old.'

They all made me think of you with your mouth half-open, adapting to a word, perpetually *trying*.

Not Yet Wednesday

This may count as sad, but I am not sorry. It's fairly safe to say that we're not talking, as in technically, with our mouths. Not even that.

What happened was: you were reading a book when I got home. You got up and gave me a face-full for not having answered all those texts. You were especially upset about one in which you'd called me 'gullet'.

'They were unanswerable,' I said.

'You would have laughed at that!' you said.

'It just means "sweetie". No one has used that word since 1970.'

The book you were reading was *Ronja Rövardotter* by Astrid Lindgren, which I think is a masterpiece, far better than *Pippi Långstrump*. It has rump hobs and ravenous birds with boobs, and now I won't get to introduce you to any of this.

'Well, great,' I said.

'Is that why you're being selfish?' you said. 'Is it about territories and pissing?'

'You didn't ask,' I said.

'You could have been smashed in the head with a bottle out there.'

'That's one thing that could have happened,' I said.

I went into the bedroom and began to get ready for bed. You started to read manhandled Astrid Lindgren words as loud as you could, and from the very middle of the book, too. I took a sock off. The truth of the matter is that you haven't told me what you think is the right thing to do either, and you think I haven't noticed that you're as far from knowing what you want as I am. I put the sock back on and you kept reading, all over the floor. It probably sounded like satanism to the neighbours. They couldn't possibly know, just like the Swedish Chef had no idea he wasn't Swedish. I couldn't decide if my feet were too hot. I took the sock off one last time and as I threw it on the mantelpiece it brushed the side of Squirrel McCamp's jar. Right then there was a bang from upstairs, someone slamming a door shut or making a point about the noise, rightly so. It made the new mouse-jar slide just a little to the left, such a fine movement that it could have been my eyelids interfering. Even though the other day you said clearly that you had a name for the mouse, there was now a Post-it-note on the jar which said: MUS.

The word for mouse is also slang for vagina and you just don't know, do you?

I laughed at you and you stopped reading. Then you said, 'You're being an arsehorse, Kristin,' quite calmly.

It's possible that when I was looking for my hair pins the other day, I unwittingly changed the position of the jars slightly, putting them in danger at some later date. McCamp is tucked in right behind said Nameless Fanny Rodent, followed closely by Elspeth the Spider and Newtongrange. I threw the other sock at them, rolled up this time, but it was still just a sock at the end of the day. Then I threw a shoe.

'That was so stupid,' you said. 'You are so fucking stupid.'

Disposing of the mouse, you leant on the palms of your hands on the cistern and stared, flushed again, and stared some more. You rubbed your lips, roughed them up disgustingly till I couldn't watch any longer. The specimen had been thoroughly contaminated.

'That was so fucking stupid,' you said.

'Are you absolutely sure it's gone now? It may float up again,' I said.

'Ignoring that you're pregnant is stupid,' you said.

You lowered the weight of your upper body, straight and shattered at the same time, onto both your hands on the cistern, as if doing a press-up.

'Arghhhhhhh!' you said.

'Gullet,' I said. 'I just got it. To you it looks like "gullet". As in mouth.'

'I can't look at you right now,' you said. 'That's how stupid.'

I went to sit on the couch. I could still watch you from over there, and I decided to only think about the Lithuanians for as long as it took you to get out of the bathroom. What would it have been like to be Daryl Urban in the year 1902 at this hour of the night? Confusing and filthy, probably, every decision capped by hunger. You looked like you were about to dive into the loo to fetch the mouse back up again and there was an asphyxiated sound lingering in the pipes. There will be issues following on from that, I'm sure. I did quite like that mouse. Every time I opened the freezer to look for peas, it was there, waiting to be given the treatment. I liked it. I especially liked the way one of its teeth was hooked over its lip, so that when it looked up at me it still put me in my place.

Fucking didn't change much, the time we first did it, but attaching the word 'fucking' to a person changes not only them but the person saying it, the one who unleashes that kind of naked unkindness.

I am a fucking something now, a fucking stupid someone.

In hindsight, it should have been worth the risk of getting my hands cut up. I could have insisted on us getting a new jar for it and doing the whole procedure again because, who knows (well, you do), it might have been possible to save it. If I'd loved you more, it wouldn't have been out of my hands.

Instead, I fell asleep for a few hours, thinking I could save Ernie by giving him mouth to mouth until he was back in the correct liquid. I have a vague memory of my mother telling me she saved a fish that way once. Half-asleep, it made sense. There was joyous music in the background, too. The bears were responsible for that.

Something else that's astonishing: a home, in Swedish, is
    en bostad   a livecity

146

And a bostadshus, for example, is a residential house. The city is in the home — an entire city already in one house. I can almost, almost see why you think compound words are worth poring over like this

eco system   ekosystem

Which is borrowed by both our languages from the Greek:

eco   home

Home-systems.

And tomorrow I was meant to make a certain call. Does it matter? What do people eat together after they've called each other stupid?

'Change has long arms,' your ma said one day, when she noticed that I'd moved the couch to the other side of the lounge. She said it approvingly, which is when I began to think that we bore her.

Wednesday

Eight am is far too late to be milking the cows, so late that sometimes they're in pain when I get there, but I'm not allowed to come in any earlier. I'll apologise and bring them pears, and this will be everything that I could possibly do for them. Pears. When new cows come in to replace the old ones, we will pretend that the ones we've come to talk about as if we knew them moved on to happier places. We'll give them new names. A while ago, a society at one of the universities joined the rest of the weekend protests on the Castle esplanade. Management wasn't keeping count of the various demands.

'Why do they all have to look the same?' Joanne Tarbuck said. 'Is there a dress code?'

The investigation into the cows' living conditions is still ongoing. Lady Gaga and Björn Skifs are doing fairly okay, I think. The rash on Björn Skifs' ear has cleared up completely.

This morning they were quite vocal. When I'd finished milking Lady Gaga, I stood up on the stool and brushed her back. She's the slightly taller one. I put away the brush and leant over with my arms across her back and down the other side. I shuffled forward and up with my toes on the stool, until I was hanging on my stomach across her back, imitating a saddle, ridiculous as neither of us know how to ride. The tension in her was seismic, the complete bafflement at a closeness so new roiling up and up. I kicked away the stool and was hung there, her torso of power and sinews, guts, against mine, pressing everything between us against my own spine and our cores against each other. Nobody talks about the calves. They don't mention how there needs to be a calf for there to be any milk. If I were Solveig, I'd know so much more about the calves.

The hours between leaving the Translation Room and being back here again are starting to swell. A whole morning has passed and look: only white space to show for it. No further texts from the livecity-house. The city, on the other hand, is working itself up to a gargantuan howl. It's called August in Edinburgh.

At long last, my belly arrived. Joanne Tarbuck looked like she'd weep whenever she came close to mentioning yesterday's debacle, the unique opportunity we'd only just missed out on because of someone's indiscretion. The strange part of that is that I don't think she suspects me. She brought the belly down to the byre when I was milking Björn Skifs, before anyone else had come in for the day.

'So,' she said. 'I found out the make of their bellies. No more than thirty quid each. They're the kind you wear with plastic braces. I'm sure they wobble around like bloody basketballs.'

She'd already hauled mine out of its box and bubble wrap, and was now extending its wings to show me how it's supposed to land on my body and engulf it.

149

'Arms up,' she said. 'Velcro here.'

She was installing it on top of the Solveig clothes.

'What are they called?' I said. 'Those huge animals with needles on their tails?'

'Bumblebees?' she said and kept tugging.

Björn Skifs wasn't pleased about any of this.

'She's getting stressed,' I said.

'Just a minute, just a minute. The cow is fine.'

She prodded and strapped. I smelt fried eggs. I thought of your head lying on my stomach when we tried to read from the same book, me pulling one single, tiny hair from it and you saying, 'What's the face you'd like on your stress ball and I'll get it for you?' The belly was hotter than I'd expected, mute and self-explanatory. It wasn't going to move for anything. I tried to sit down on the milking stool again with the belly on, and found that there wasn't enough space.

'This isn't going to work right now,' I said. 'I have to finish first or she'll get sick.'

'Well now,' Joanne Tarbuck said. 'Pregnant Vikings milked, too, didn't they?'

'How would you know?'

'Pardon?'

'I mean, tell me more about pregnant Vikings, please.'

She pressed her hands together for a little stretch of the arms. I bet she swims and that she wears a swimming cap, without fail, every Tuesday at seven.

'I'll give you some material to read at the end of the day.'

'A stingray!' I said. 'That's what I was thinking about.'

150

I would love for someone to break down in front of me right now and just *tell* me what it's like.

'It feels like I can't take it off,' I said.

'That's very good,' she said. 'I'm sure that's what we want.'

I asked if I could finish up here and then put it on properly, underneath the shift rather than on top of it, like I was selling ice cream on a beach. Björn Skifs was headbanging and her right eye was rolling counter-clockwise. Lady Gaga was looking nervous, too. It was only understandable, what with Joanne Tarbuck's smell of bohemian scarf-shop.

'We need to be one step ahead,' she said. 'I haven't brought this up with management yet, but there are a few ways we could progress. Let me say this. There are alternatives. Creative ones.'

She winked, then left, and I milked Björn Skifs who had begun to thunder. When you put a hand against a cow's flank, it seems like her whole body is a bag of liquids mixed together and bubbling. They make the soundtrack of bad weather when they're uneasy. They sound like a

stämmsång   voice/tune-song

a song in parts, performed by guts and several stomachs.

I cleaned out their boxes and only then I realised that Joanne Tarbuck had been speaking English to me this whole time. And that Solveig had spoken English back. The cows had both heard it happen. It was like remembering that you've left your bed in the middle of the night, but only once you see your sleepy face in the bathroom mirror — all that unconscious mileage. I hid the belly behind the grain sacks, way in there, along with Algot's warrior things.

At around nine fifty I left Ingrid and Algot to their pretend-skinning of two rabbits and went down to Argyle Battery. At work I use the watch your ma gave me, but I've only kept the face so that I can hide it in a second. Three times in the last few days, I thought I'd lost it and I decided to call her to apologise, then tell her about Project, because what the hiccup, we're on the subject of lost time anyway. Then I found the watch again.

The Castle is frying today, oily sunshine reaching all the way in on the cobbled stones, in between hairs on scalps. When I was passing the new barracks someone yelled 'suck my fika'. He sounded out of breath, poor French guy. It's stressful to break laws in broad daylight.

'Visste du att femton procent av Storbrittaniens befolkning är ansvariga för sjuttio procent av alla flygresor?'	'Did you know that fifteen percent of the UK's population take seventy percent of all flights?'

I yelled back.

They have no idea, but as long as it's Swedish it might as well be the truth.

Algot is worried that the fika nonsense will go on for as long as there are people to remember what happened at the Parade. He would know. In school he once made the mistake of thinking that a compass was a form of contraception and was bullied for three years. He told me about this whilst shovelling some random dirt for the benefit of a Canadian family who were watching us. They told us they lived in a town in upstate New York called Valhalla.

152

None of the Lithuanians seemed to be above ground. There was a line of tourists going down into the mines, most of them with something eatable in one hand — as if they'd be gone for hours — and a phone at the ready in the other. This is good news for the Lithuanians. At nine fifty-eight I finally spotted Daryl Urban, rushing across the battery from the direction of the gates. He stopped at the first cannon to tie his shoe laces, just as Mr Crossley, a.k.a. Phil, arrived from the opposite direction. They met close to the mine-opening but didn't give each other as much as a nod.

For about twenty seconds they stood there, not talking. I was pretending to read the plaque on the wall of one of the Lithuanian village houses. I know it said that the Cart Shed buildings were used in the 1700s after the Jacobite risings, so I must not have been pretending after all. Daryl Urban and Mr Crossley began to fidget and wander about, each avoiding the other's pathway. Daryl sneaked a glance at a watch. They were waiting for the moment when it would become unscripted that they stood there, together, and they'd have to do something else to justify it. Watching it was like staying inside the second after you touch something burning, before it hurts. No one else had shown up.

'What's a Swedish Pokémon called?' this woman yelled.

'Fika-choo!' was the answer.

A few feet away was the box on which Daryl Urban's wife was supposed to stand to deliver her speech after their planned re-enactment. Daryl and Mr Crossley started fiddling with their hats, flattening caps, flicking balls of stray fabric off their lapels.

More time fell and died, and if they decided when it was time to give up, I missed the moment the decision was made. They left so easily, again without looking at each other, Mr Crossley to the docks and Daryl down into the black hole. They didn't even wait ten minutes for anyone else to keep their promise.

I turned around to go back and bumped into a rubbish bin. Immediately, I put a hand on the belly to comfort the area of impact. Someone found that hilarious.

'Du får prata precis hur du vill!'	'You're allowed to speak just the way you like!'

I yelled to them and watched them assume things about this, too.

In the armchair, in the tower, the belly looks like a big, foreign holiday.

'Maybe they saw someone coming,' you'd say if I told you about the Lithuanians.

'Nah, there was no one coming, Bobe. They just decided it wasn't worth it.'

'Maybe they knew something you didn't.'

'Maybe you should explain yourself.'

A thing you've always done: you hold up my selfishness and undress it to the tiniest hair without knowing that's what you're doing. It's repulsive, really.

'I'm thinking in the wrong direction,' you said some time ago, when we were out looking for a delivery office. I offered

154

to check a map.

'Mr Innes shat himself today, when he was trying to finish a crossword.'

I should have listened to the story, but I needed to make sure we weren't also getting lost in that horrid industrial estate.

'I was cleaning him up, right? Fucking insipid music on the radio he had on and I couldn't stop thinking about how humiliating it all was. I mean for *me*. His taste in music, the way he talks about India. The more we flushed and wiped.'

'You had to feel something. You didn't tell him you didn't like his music, did you?'

'It's already a pretty small shower he's got. I couldn't breathe and it wasn't even the smell. He just smelt like the really strong shampoo he uses. Aloe vera or some such. There just wasn't any space. I was scrubbing his arse and I still wasn't thinking about him. He might as well not have been in there.'

'What do people talk about when they're being showered anyway?' I said.

The way I was imagining it, he was singing along. We were not on the right identical street now. We were definitely not getting closer.

'He looked at the wall. Then when I left, he thanked me. Which is hideous when you really don't deserve it.'

You were squashing the sides of your eyes. Is it racist that I sometimes look at you and don't think I see the difference in our colours? Is it bad that I just see you, and that it isn't a colour? I was thinking about being out of breakfast cereal.

frukostflingor　　　　　　breakfast flakes

but not all cereals are flakes. That, right there, is probably what you meant by 'thinking in the wrong direction'. What I was just doing. Listening is a full-time job.

In Swedish it's

göra en abort   to make an abortion

What an activity.

If that woman standing with her buggy in the middle of Crown Square looks up at the tower before I can count to ten, then I'll choose in the next five minutes. I will make an abortion. It will be round and designed, made primarily out of silicone. We will stay here. If the rook (which by the way moves like a porn star and whose feathers reminds me of my father's sideburns) on top of the barracks remains on the same section of roof for the next thirty seconds, then I will have it. Then I'll be pregnant. If you say 'hi' in your own voice when I come home and offer me a bag of crisps — if they are salt and balsamic vinegar crisps — then we'll stay the same. We'll find useful ways of talking rubbish. *We* will be okay.

And what then, of everyone else?

Here: there is a text from you, the first one today, and I don't open it.

Instead I find another old email from you. It's the one where you told me about how you thought HIV was an airline until you were twelve, and that you wouldn't accept that adults weren't all the same age. Piled up, this will keep me going until about closing time.

Joanne Tarbuck is right, the belly really is of a superior quality. It doesn't bounce or slip around in the slightest, but it does expand my crashable area beyond the usual and into other people's remit. It takes practice to handle that kind of girth. There is just that bit more reach, especially where corners are concerned. If I were Solveig I would feel it, all the way out there, every single tickle, every burn and stretch.

I was rearranging steatite bowls in the corner of the dwelling-house, thinking I was alone in there. Then I turned around and bumped Ingrid out of balance. I wanted to offer an arm to steady her, but the belly slowed me down until it wasn't necessary anymore.

'I've been using it as a tray,' I said.

Ingrid pointed at it and said something to Algot.

'Tell her I knew she wouldn't like it,' I said. 'That was just never going to happen.'

'She'd like to pinch it,' Algot said.

'Are you high?' I said.

Algot hunched.

'That's what she said.'

Ingrid put down the bowl she was holding and stepped closer. She did a little shimmy, as if after a fresh breeze. She has three kids and from what I hear they're all politicians. She had them in the nineties. I tried to remember the things people might have found unreal in the nineties.

'What's "pinch" in Icelandic?' I said. 'If you're taking the piss I won't swap your Christmas shifts.'

'Klipa,' said Ingrid.

'Sounds like the Swedish word for rock,' I said, just making conversation.

Her approach was making me nervous. Ingrid is the closest thing Solveig would have to a doctor and a midwife. She would have done much more than pinching as things progressed. We sneaked in behind one of the pillars. There was a receipt from the ticket office on the floor, folded across a piece of gum. I lifted my pinafore and shift, standing with my back to the entrance. Algot stood guard, humming about storms and the most famous battles.

'Look out for cameras,' I yelled.

She wetted her lips and nodded. Her hand spread out for a wide grab, then it focused in, her forefinger and thumb extending and her other fingers crooking back into her palm. It looked like it was about to snuff out a flame. She squeezed the piglet-coloured surface into a peak, held it for a moment, then let it sink again without so much as a rivulet. It kept its shape wonderfully.

Algot needed to go and do the thing where he stands at the entrance and preaches about the promises of riches further down south. If inspiration doesn't strike on a particular day, he often takes to reciting Norwegian Eurovision lyrics. Ingrid pinched the belly again, harder. This time a bit more silicone gave way and then bounced back. Her face was taut with tiny strangers.

'That *would* have hurt,' I said.

Golly, some people just don't knock.

'Stäng gärna dörren efter dig,'	'Do please close the door behind you,'

158

I said to the back of a tourist, because there is no door.

'I don't care, by the way,' I said to Ingrid. 'I don't care that you told people.'

She carefully folded down my clothes over the belly, then briefly held a hand on top of the fabric. I was thinking that we would have made predictions together, about what wild beasts, wild waterfalls, and wild people would do to the project in there. Would we study the colour of my urine? Solveig would ask her about everything, and there would be nothing she wouldn't know. Then, when all of that was over, I'd look after her in her old age. Ingrid rushed her hand away, moved it to her own left breast and cupped it.

'Woah,' I said and checked that bacon-woman was gone.

Ingrid cleared her throat. Now she was cradling the breast. Then she pointed at the belly again.

'Sama,' she said.

Which sounded like

samma   same

'Krabbamein,' she said and looked at me with her eyes almost closed.

'I don't know what that means,' I said.

'Krabbamein,' she said again and squeezed past me out of the corner.

krabba   sounds like crab

a krabba is similar to a kräfta   cray fish

att ha kräftan, *they used to say*   to have cancer

'Jesus,' I said. 'What about now? Are you okay now?'

She didn't answer.

159

'Ingrid,' I said. 'Is it over?'

'That's always what they want to know,' Algot translated from the other side of the wall, where he must have been having a piss.

So much of all this has never happened before.

My mother sends me film recommendations every couple of weeks. They are the most thoughtful thing. She thinks I'd like the shots of reindeer and forests in this one. Apparently, the film, which is Russian and called *Cuckoo*, is about a Finnish and a Soviet soldier during WWII who become stranded with a Sami woman in her hut when one of them is injured. Throughout the film, none of the three characters understand a word of what any of the others are saying, and that is it. That's the film.

'Jag tänkte på dig och ditt jobb,'	'I thought about you and your work,'

my mum says.

They are the most thoughtful thing, although not always in the way she means it.

'Ni kanske kan titta på den tillsammans,'	'Maybe you could watch it together,'

she adds.

Oh man, maybe we could have.

Every time Ingrid does this one particular ritual, she uses the opportunity to try to impart actual knowledge to us. It will be something about the reason why her staff is curved in this way, for example, or about the role of the völva in the interaction between pre-Christian and Christian societies. This afternoon, when I got to the spot, Ingrid and Algot were standing each on one side of the fence, half-yelling at each other, then whispering one or two words and then almost yelling again. It was much more noticeable than if they'd just talked in a regular tone of voice. Algot said she was being immature.

'Joanne Tarbuck wants her to perform a ceremony involving birth runes. For Solveig's baby.'

'Oh,' I said.

'She's going on about how there's no research to tell us what such a ceremony would have been like. Well make it up then, mother dear.'

Ingrid gesticulated toward three children watching us.

'If she doesn't do it that's bad news for all of us. I don't have time for this, not now. I need the overtime and you don't get overtime unless you do the work.'

'Can't you just sing, Ingrid?' I said.

She shook her head.

'Just a bit. We could paint on the belly, that would look good.'

'Yeah,' said Algot, but he was looking at me like something wasn't quite right with me either.

Ingrid went inside the dwelling-house and sat on the dirt floor, by the hearth. She dug the staff hard into the earth between her legs, but although she was clearly upset, I don't think she meant to break it. I wanted her to read things over me.

'She came by earlier,' said Algot.

'It could be a happy thing,' I said.

'She wants to see you. Again.'

'Who?' I said.

'Seriously?' said Algot. 'You ask?'

I did send you a message, just to let you know I'd be late again. You did not answer. Not knowing where to go from there, I opened one of the messages you sent earlier. It wasn't what I was looking for at all. At the time it was written, a certain rodent was still un-dead.

Oddly, Joanne Tarbuck pretended she wasn't expecting me. At first, I thought: not this again. It was so typical it stung. Then I tried, at least, to think she had forgotten, or that she'd just had some bad news. She opened the door with her nostrils fluttering, wearing a period dress with ruffles. Iron Maiden was coming out of her desktop speakers and the room was full of crumpet smell.

'Are you going to be a historical person, too?' I said.

She sniffed and waved at me to sit down. The desk had been moved back to its original position by the window. She rolled back and forth on her desk chair for about a minute. My chair didn't have any wheels on it.

'Apparently not,' she said. 'Apparently, those of us who aren't bilingual or trilingual or whatever aren't allowed to have the fun jobs. Apparently, we're only good for paperwork and for managing you lot day in and day out.'

'Managing?' I said.

'It's okay. Nothing to do with you,' she said.

'It looks good on you,' I said.

'Did you know I graduated with a first in history? I always thought I was going to do research. I had the grades. But, that's how it goes.'

She picked up a paperweight in the shape of the Castle and put it down again, very slowly, like landing a helicopter on a fly. The breast-part and the shoulder-part of the dress squeezed her flesh all up and together and made her rise above her neckline. If she were dough she would have burned by now.

'Eighteenth-century French aristocracy,' she said. 'But no bother. They've said no because I don't speak bloody French well enough.'

'I always did think of French as bloody,' I said.

'That's it for now,' she said.

I almost got up, but she waved at me to remain seated.

'I behaved very unprofessionally earlier, down in the byre. I did realise that you'd already been to your Translation Room. I shouldn't have spoken to you. In my defence, I felt like, at the time, it was more important to communicate with you than to follow policy.'

I said that was fine. Being here, I thought, being here and fine, is still a dream isn't it?

'I made it difficult for you to do your job. I was very excited, and a little angry about the whole prosthetic abdomen thing. I do apologise for putting you in a difficult position by speaking to you in English while on duty.'

'It's all in the past,' I actually said.

'You could, of course, have replied to me in Swedish anyway. You can always do that. At least then you will have done your bit and you'll have done nothing wrong, if it comes to it. You will have followed the rules.'

It was quiet for a moment. The music had stopped and so had the rolling of the chair.

'Comes to what?' I said.

'Don't be daft, Kirsten. Not like that. I'm merely theorising. It is healthy for us to revisit these issues from time to time. Do you want a fika, then?'

'Fick you,'

I didn't say.

She sat down in her gown just as if women through the ages had never ever had trouble breathing in that kind of outfit.

'Say, hypothetically,' she said, 'that we were to hire a baby. How would you feel about being its mother?'

But okay, I thought, hypothetically we could do a million things.

'I can't guarantee we'd pay you more because of it, but I'm not saying no either. We would have to look at what kind of growth it brings, profit margins. You could see it as the possibility of a bonus if it goes well.'

'How would you? Hire?' I said.

'Commercials hire babies all the time. TV shows, films. We would obviously pay its parents.'

'Wouldn't the baby's parents have to be with the baby?'

I remember hundreds of times when my mother complained about troublesome children in the plays she'd been in, and the more troublesome parents following the kids everywhere. She said all child actors' parents live vicariously, which is why I was never allowed to go into acting. They were afraid of their own insecurities, which is a thing about them I'm happily reminded of sometimes.

'Certainly,' said Joanne Tarbuck, 'I have a few ideas.'

'Oh no,' I said.

'It's fine, have a biscuit.'

'No, sorry, what was your idea?'

'I was thinking we could hire someone with a child, and she or he could be Solveig's and Sigurd's slave. We'd obviously not use the word "slave". We might call them "serfs". People like Sigurd and Solveig most likely had two or so.'

'Would they most likely have beaten them, too?' I said.

'Oh, come on. You think Solveig would have dug her own loo?'

'She was supposed to be normal.'

'And have a ship to come over from Norway?'

'Who would they be?' I said. 'I mean, what would they speak?'

'Picts most likely. But Picts are a sensitive subject. We'd probably say they arrived with you. She'd be in the room all the time and that would make it legal, with the baby.'

She said 'she', like there was already someone lined up.

'This is strictly between us two. I don't want Daniel getting wind of it. There will be brainstorming sessions, but they'll be strictly by invitation only. The house needs some restoration work anyway. We'll have a crib built in time for next season.

We have to take the long view with this, *Kirsten*.'

Fick you, I thought again and didn't say. Apart from all the rest, you're also capable of lifting one eyebrow and not the other. All of this, and you probably feel sorry for yourself. I reminded her of how I'd already been working here for a full year after graduating. I told her I couldn't imagine working anywhere else, which was absolutely true.

'But this is not happening till next year?' I said. 'It's just that the belly might make it warmer during the winter.'

'The Lithuanians,' she said. 'You can see how I'm worried? They have this need to always be first at everything. So. If you get to wear that thing through the winter, then you're in?'

'Joanne Tarbuck,'

I didn't say.

'Joanne Tarbuck, I'm about to ask you an economic question, and I know I've never asked you an economic question before.'

She looked truly exhausted.

'I thought there was no budget for new Peoples,' I said. 'But there's money for this?'

'Pet,' she said, 'that's a question for Finance.'

Which wasn't her, which wasn't either of us.

Her phone rang shortly after that, and I stood up.

'What? Again?' she said into it. 'Well she'll have gone to see Mr Innes down the road.'

I waved goodbye at her, but she held out her hand and pointed to my chair.

'Stay,' she mouthed.

166

'Well. What? Have you checked the wee Scotmid on Easter Road? Yes, you, checking it. You should have been there half an hour ago anyway. Ask them. What? Well tell them to look out for an eighty-six-year-old woman in a glittery dress. Jesus.'

Jesus, indeed. Bleedy hell, Bobe. There you are. I was just thinking in the wrong direction and there you are again.

'Jesus Christ. Are you going? Are you on your way now? I want to know that you're checking now. She'll be there or with Mr Innes. Honest to god, if you don't find her right now, I'm calling the office.'

After hanging up, she looked at me. It was hard to smile back, with it being so clear just then that we had no idea what to do with each other. The colour green is probably not even green to her.

I said: 'Have you ever been pregnant?'

She looked out the window at the precise moment when two pigeons collided in a mad embrace, then precipitated out of the picture. She jumped and said 'Jesus Christ!' again. I held my breath and counted the days since this thing started. She looked at me and rolled her eyes.

'It didn't really qualify,' she said. 'I realised very early that it wasn't going to be right.'

'Did you feel like, you know, it was the wrong time?'

'Well this has turned serious.'

'Never mind,' I said.

'I was in a weird mood yesterday,' she said.

She got up and so did I.

'I think my partner possibly takes care of your mother,' I

said.

'Pardon me?'

'He works for the council.'

'Oh,' she said. 'Oh man.'

'They love him. He's the brown, short person who never ever asks for help.'

'Please leave.'

'He's funny. He's so afraid of making mistakes.'

I wanted to tell her about the glittery dress, the one in which an old lady, at the time not so old, had met Jimmy Savile, and that I still have it, that we haven't forgotten about it or stolen it, but she just kept saying: 'Oh man' and blushing until I was out. My parents are at home this week. They're in between things, which means in between jobs, not doing much except tidying and worrying about rent. It's not really worrying anymore, though, my dad says, when you're in your late fifties, it's more like a slow meditation on dust. I know he's lying. I texted my mum to let her know I'll call tomorrow and to thank her for the film recommendation. I didn't say that I'd looked it up and it's fairly impossible to get hold of. I also said I needed to talk to her about something that would take approximately twenty minutes.

| 'Nej men, gumman, vad har hänt?' | 'No but, little old lady, what has happened?' |

Don't ever literally translate the things your parents have called you your whole life — even as a joke. It'll crush you.

If I were Solveig: when I left my country, my voice would never

168

again be heard by those still in that country. I would never again be reached by theirs. No video calls in the Viking age as far as we're aware, unless you count inhabiting the minds of birds and going on excursions with them.

to stay in touch doesn't mean   what it claims to mean

I would have been terminally in one place, with not much choice but to be fine with that place, whatever that is on a certain day, and to not trash it.

I might have been one of the people who don't leave because they feel like it (a change of environment, trying on a new public transport system), but because they're forced to. I might have run away from too little or too much of something monstrous, and my only choices were leaving or dying, if they're always that mutually exclusive.

If the Future happened now: touch might return to the hands. When the quick connections crash and separation becomes itself again, will we have chosen where we are?

Time to go home now. Grab a bag of crisps, for that idea in there with the hunger, and then go home.

On another Wednesday

a few years ago, we made our first preservation together. I was possibly still drunk from having discovered Lagavulin the night before. Its accent was still all over my tongue:

'Window open?' I'm sure you said.

'Well excuse *me*,' I said.

'Your breath has got nothing on the formaldehyde, K-bot,' you said. 'Gloves on?'

'Sure,' I said.

'Ow!'

'Sorry,' I said. 'I thought we were in a hurry.'

'Do you have somewhere to be?' you said.

'See,' I said, 'that's a very good question.'

Obviously, I'd rather have been in bed, but ideally with you in it, as well. Wednesdays, at the time, were preservation-work days without fail and I'd been sent a formal invitation.

'Your mask isn't on properly,' you said. 'Fix it now or you're out before you know it.'

'Who's the lizard?' I said and poked at it with one of our three forks.

'It's a great crested newt,' you said. 'We'll name him when

170

he's done. Now hold this.'

Its tiny eyes were fogged over, neither open nor closed, but replaced with matter. Lying on its back, its dinosaur tail melted into the towel like something already composted. Its belly was full of inkblots. Your ma had found it on one of her longer hikes. She kept it in a carrier bag on two buses and three trains home, full of muck and water. She drinks beer for her nerves when she travels, so people may have thought the bog smell was coming from her.

'Christ,' I said. 'How do they make it so deliciously smoky like that?'

My tongue. This was when I started with the hip flask.

You injected the newt all over, squirting formalin into its eyes and even into its mandatory smile. This, I thought, I'm going to find fascinating in a moment, I'll start finding it fascinating really soon, but until then: oh. It was something about the distance between the wee guy and the way you went at it, brutally in control, every touch of the needle putting you more in charge until the animal was all bloated.

'What's the difference between conservation and preservation?' I asked.

I thought about the faces you'd wipe and despise a little and wipe anyway, because you'd decided again and again to care for a living.

To care:

att ta hand om   to take in hand

The dead newt was in both your hands. This was not what I thought your caring might look like.

171

'I think,' you said, 'preserving is more about the dead and conserving is for corals. I think.'

'Thank you for coming,' you said.

That hot teacher of yours back in high school has so much to answer for.

But see, that doesn't work out either because:

konservburk   tin can

Unless in Sweden they use tin cans for living things and I just never noticed. Certain kinds of fermented fish, I suppose, might qualify.

You choose the worst times to talk about food. Twice in half an hour now, you'd mentioned a craving for turkey dinosaurs. It's best just to ask you a question and see if that changes anything.

'What's the most difficult thing you've tried to preserve?' I said.

'Banana peel,' you said. 'I tried it with a lot of food when I was a teenager, but it didn't really work. I used to sneak away bits of dinner but then I stopped when my mum started bringing books about eating disorders to the flat.'

'It won't look the same though,' I said, feeling sick. 'Will it? The orange especially.'

In the beginning, I couldn't get enough of hearing you say the word 'food'. Fudd. With a snappy 'd' like no one saw it coming. Scottish accents were a guilty novelty for so long, and especially, obviously, yours. Newt. Food. Soot. What a treat to be part of that — different snaps at the end — to have arrived.

And it's still Wednesday now

Midnight, Translation Room. It's really fucking freezing. And, no, we're not bothering with the tidiness which a little 'i' brings anymore.

The plan, as it was, included surprising you with a brand-new mood, by coming in around the back of the building. I was going to climb in through the bathroom window, the way we did a few times when we first moved in and the flat below was empty. After that, the plan would go something like:

'Hey, Bobe, let's sit down and say things with each other. The way we do.'

You'd say: 'Yeah sure, K-watt, let me put some trousers on first.'

I'd tell you to go ahead and let them be, if you were wearing the Christmas pants.

There was someone smoking outside the front of the house, a girl with a thin neck. I wondered if people sometimes talked to her about Anne Boleyn without realising why. I had to ask her to move twice so I could get past, and even then, she left me so little space that I had to squeeze right through an overpowering smell of fry-up. I decided to start with this, once I had you sat

173

down and ready to go. It would be a fact, and neutral.

The back garden was very blue, with even bluer ribbons around it where the bushes belong in daylight. All of Tall Azif's socks were on the washing line, by themselves, as if holding the space for fatter friends. There was that time we climbed up the back and you lost it because you found a blood stain on the wall where no blood had reason to go.

It was much harder to get up there now than I remembered. Pretty much straight away, my arms began to tremble at the elbows, my wrists unlocking themselves from the rest of the arm. Solveig would never be afraid of heights. I bet she would have been tied up somewhere high as a toddler just for fun. It would have been a formative experience for her. My feet kept growing as I got further off the ground and I only just made it up to the bathroom window before one of them slipped. I banged my forehead against the windowsill, heard someone swearing, and it was me.

I don't really know why, but I wasn't expecting you to be having a wee just *then* either.

'Fuckin' hell!' you shouted and pulled your trousers up.

I looked the other way until you were done. It seemed like the best thing considering how desolate your bum looked suddenly, oddly square. There were nice remnants of formalin in the air, though.

'There's a girl out there who smells like a fry-up and I think it's just the way she smells,' I said.

You'd had a shave. There was more of your face all in all

and nothing wrong with that, according to the plan.

'What the hell are you doing?' you said.

'Surprising,' I said. 'Rising from the surp. What is a surp anyway?'

'It's almost nine,' you said. 'Although I guess that's early for you nowadays? To come home?'

'You sound excellent,' I said. 'You just sound right.'

'Yeah,' you said, 'I was always going to take a break right about now anyway. If that matters to you.'

'Ask me why the window,'

I didn't say.

'I wanted to see what you look like when I'm not here,'

I didn't say either.

If I were Solveig: aged twenty-four, I might not even qualify as young anymore, and I might not have been running for anything like my life — possibly, I was just put off over some inheritance, a pissy relative. Possibly, it was easier to cross the sea than to stay and have an awkward family meeting. Either way, having the kid posed the lesser risk of disappearance.

You went to the bedroom. How you and how predictable. That's where they all are, with their minuscule bullet eyes to back you up.

'I had a meeting with Joanne Tarbuck,' I said. 'I'm being promoted, in a way.'

'I thought Joanne Tarbuck was supposed to be a selfish posho.'

'You know I'm pretty sure I've never said that about her,' I said. 'You didn't go to work today either, did you?'

'I did. Like I told you I would. Mr Innes wanted his nails painted and we timed it in under five minutes.'

You held up one green-tipped finger. The shades in your eyes rattled. The jars were there and they are someone's pals.

You said: 'I'm so tired of waiting for you to bring it up when it feels like you never will.'

'Well,' I said. 'At some point I would have. It's how it works, or doesn't, depending.'

'Look in the mirror,' you said.

I got up. I looked like a racoon.

'Can you please tell me if you think you're healthy?'

'Did you know that people often get odd cravings around week eleven?' I said. 'I feel like eating that white kind of bark you see on some trees. Is that birch?'

'I, well,' you said. 'There's probably a recipe somewhere.'

People hardly ever say: I am deciding or We are changing now. When it's time to talk about it, the crossing of a line, we're always already there, if we have survived. The way you sighed made me want to grab your head and dislodge something you could spit out.

'Tell me about when you first got here,' I said.

'Got where, K?'

'You remember an airplane window. Maybe you could see the wing, and someone working on the tarmac as well.'

'The building works?' you said. 'Those finished last week. I

176

spoke to the guy with the mohawk down on the corner.'

'And the shoes,' I said. 'What shoes were you wearing on the plane?'

'What on earth,' you said, 'are you talking about?'

'When you arrived, Bobe. In Scotland.'

'Jesus,' you said. 'I don't fucking know and that's without the headache.'

You were pulling at your own thumbs.

'You remembered your mum speaking to you and you didn't understand.'

'Whatever,' you said. 'I was trying to be proactive. What have you done?'

'She wasn't your mum and then she was. I'm interested in when that happened.'

'Kristin, if I told you there was a fire out there right now, how much would you actually give a fuck?'

'I'm thinking that maybe I want to keep it.'

'Woah,' you said.

You stood up but lost your balance and ended up on the floor.

'I was wearing blue trainers,' you said and then you tried to touch my foot.

'People do it all the time,' I said. 'Even the ones who read the news, even people like us do.'

This was when you began to move your shoulders in circles. Could be that your arms had fallen asleep, both of them and at the same time.

177

'You want to keep it?' you said. 'You're saying you want to actually keep it.'

'I've been thinking that. Maybe yes.'

'Kristin.'

'Yup,' I said.

'Nah,' you said.

Round and round. They would have fallen off if I hadn't attacked them. I held your arms down for one minute and thirteen seconds. It was very comforting and it wasn't enough. You were breathing so loud it came out through your ears. You'll be okay at playing and fantastic at teaching. They will have your ears.

'Inappropriate,' I said and you let go, head nodding, nodding.

'We have psychopathic governments,' you said. 'A mega methane fucking burp about to happen in Siberia. I can't bring someone into this.'

'You were watching a war zone the other night and you didn't even blink,' I said. 'I saw you. It was like looking at someone performing boob surgery.'

'I told you, I was working. You want us to have a kid now? You think that's the right thing to do?'

'If you don't want it,' I said, 'what the fuck was the deal with the lessons?'

'I wanted to be useful,' you said.

'Nah,' I said. 'That's not it.'

'Well it should be.'

'You're just scared,' I said.

'I wanted to know.'

'And?' I said.

'I wanted to handle—'

'Bingo!' I said.

I grabbed my phone. Out of all things I grabbed my phone, and touched *that* instead.

What if they were born with your short legs and my long arms, they may end up looking funny and it's not going to be much fun for them. If I were Solveig, I might have asked for spells from my mother-in-law to prevent that kind of accident. There would be ways and tools. But for now:

'You didn't know how to tell your ma you were thirsty. She didn't understand what you were saying because you were speaking Portuguese and you were three years old.'

'Christ.'

'And then at some point she did, and you did, too, and that was the new normal.'

'Why?' you said.

'Just, please,' I said.

'You know what? All I remember is an advert on the back of the seat. Palm trees, and someone holding an ugly kind of pink cocktail. It's fine. Being from somewhere else has never been a problem, K, what happens now is the problem.'

'It must have happened, though. You get on the plane, and then you get off, and at some point, she becomes your ma. Or maybe after that? Do you remember anything from the airport?'

'I have to tell you now,' you said. 'I can't see it.'

'I know,' I said. 'It was a long time ago.'

'I can't see it, like. It being okay.'

'I'm really sorry about the mouse,' I said.

'It just looked so fucking lonely on the floor.'

You went over and checked that nobody was balancing precariously.

'Ciaran,' I said.

'It's the worst time,' you said.

'Fuck you,' I said. 'Fuck you for not just saying that a week ago.'

'Will you just stop swearing? It doesn't go well with you.'

'It does,' I said. 'Fuck fuck fuck you for leaving me alone.'

I told you I was going for a walk. You went into the bathroom and I had this thought that maybe your knees were going to break away as you walked, like you were in a cartoon. Knobbly knees like yours, dry elephant knees when you shower too much, and you always shower too much because you worry about contaminating the old people with a thousand conditions. The old people worry about all your showers. I looked around, really frustrated about something or other. I just couldn't catch what it was and swallow it. Then I got it. I was looking for a mouse, and the reason I was annoyed was because there was none.

Wednesday night

Two am.

You said it's the Future's fault for being a horror film.

If I were Solveig, this would be the Future.

Does that help, I mean, at all?

Barbara sometimes does extra hours as a night guard. I didn't really think she'd let me back in at half past ten and when she did, with not much but a gaze at the time, a sneeze, I wondered what she does take seriously. We're all on zero-hour contracts; if someone finds out, she *will* lose her job. This didn't stop me from asking her to do it. I told her I really needed to read a book on digs in Shetland which Ingrid had put aside for me in the museum library.

'You know Ingrid,' I said. 'You know what she's like. She won't stop nagging until I've memorised the right findings.'

'You guys are always so strange,' she said. 'Just call her Ursula. That's her name, isn't it? The one with like a million grandchildren?'

'I thought you wanted to have your own exhibition?' I said.

I honestly had been about to say 'be one of us'. She rolled her eyes.

'Camera three is out of order,' she said. 'You might want

to be aware.'

I nodded at her black eye, which she didn't have the other day when we arranged the brochures. It happened at a gig, she said. She'd managed to get to the front row in spite of some massive guy's relentless elbow. She swore she'd felt the singer's sweat on her lips.

The cleaner doesn't even come up here every other day. I think she's supposed to but has a poorly back. Once, I found a used tampon under the armchair, wrapped in a page of *The Skinny*. It was a page full of album reviews, and I read a couple of lines before admitting that I was still staring at someone's used tampon. The string was hanging out like a thin white tail. 'Excuse me, excuse me for coming next,' it said. There are dust bunnies falling straight off the TV screen, no excuses whatsoever.

dammråttor   dust rats

One question could be: which best describes the dead bits of human?

If I were Solveig: somewhere there's a millionth of a dust rat left of me.

I hardly ever see the other Translation Room users. There's this Spanish girl who wears her hair in a braid as long as her arm and really heavy eye make-up. It makes her look caught out at all times. One morning last year, when I was running late, I bumped into this Russian guy in the stairwell. Later, I found out that he's not actually Russian, even in a hand-me-down sense. He spent three years planning to marry someone and move to St Petersburg. Then he got dumped and got a job here instead.

This is the place where they sit, holding on to their jobs, being grateful for their jobs, tearing into their jobs, sometimes doing their jobs, wanting away, the fuck away from their jobs. If you're only in a place when you're alone, is it your place alone?

Two thirty am.

Something: there was a sound, a wee yelp, as if a child had been make-believe frightened, by someone helping it get rid of hiccups. I lifted the curtain flap just an inch, but it was way too dark to make out any details on the square. The lights from the city are buzzling, until your eyes get tired of all that difference and water them all down to one loud blast.

There: there was the sound again. Squee and flee.

Someone down there could either be in need of help or they could be in stitches. I can't tell if I should go check. Should I go check? If I check, they might see me. There would be some sort of conversation, exhausting, maybe good.

That was it, then. It's gone. There's no need to go and check.

Three am.

I went and I checked.

There's a torch we keep up here in case of emergencies. In the same cupboard, I found a bag of rubber bands, all tidy and unused, as well as a small note saying, 'PICK UP HIS MEDS'. When I opened the front door downstairs, there was the thud of someone running off, unnervingly close by. They must have been standing right outside. I shut it, thought about all the good people, and when I reopened it there was the back of a denim jacket in full trot across the square. They were wearing very dark trousers, so the jacket looked like it was bouncing on its very own, three feet above the ground. Some other people were on the opposite side, one of them leaning, broad-legged, over what looked like a huge, white bag. The way their elbows were pressed against their sides, holding tight and moving back and forth, looked like it could be for work. No one seemed to be hurting anyone else, so I shut the door again.

'How is it possible for all of this to be this old?' I would have said to you.

'I'm only calling security because if I don't, and something goes to shit, it will be my fault,' I would have said.

Barbara's colleague, Justice, had no idea about anything. She does capoeira and that's pretty much all I know about her. She didn't believe me when I said there were people working on something on Crown Square, in fact, she was annoyed that I was calling her when she was in the middle of watching some series. I would have guessed horror, from just listening to her. Her sentences are so sharp you have to be out like a rocket in between.

'Are you going to come and kick me out?' I said.

I didn't mean to sound flirty.

'Oh, grow up,' she said, 'just don't make me leave my hut.'

She hung up. I could no longer hear any of the voices outside.

When the Castle was bought up, they wanted to move across all pertinent material from the National Museum of Scotland. Ingrid worked there for a while. She insinuated that there's some bad blood, to do with funding and entrance fees. As a result, we only have the one Viking display, filled with the objects found in one female grave from Westray. There used to be a door between the entrance and the Palace Halls, where the artefacts are kept, but they took it down to treat rot a year ago and it never went back up. We're not supposed to wander around the indoor exhibitions. Living history next to the dead one, chewing gum, curdles the experience. As a result, I don't get to see her a lot. Her left-overs.

That is her, arranged on wee purple cushions:

Some human bones, female.

A necklace of forty assorted beads.

An Irish brooch pin from the eighth century.

(The scalp under that, somewhere under that, might have itched until it bled.)

Various tools: heckles, shears, fragment from a bowl, part of a knife, etc, etc.

A pair of bronze tortoise brooches, of the kind you find all over the Viking world. Solveig's plastic ones are modelled after these. A couple of times I've seen Ingrid sneak in to dust off the Westray case and inspect the artefacts, even though it's not even close to her responsibility. She has a thing for the specific which never left with retirement.

(The collarbones, possibly bruised, somewhere under all of that.)

Some more human bones, etc.

Almost certainly an infant's, etc, etc.

In 1963, a couple of men on Rosay, Orkney, were about to bury a cow when they found the brooches first. The grave, we're told, belonged to an affluent Norse woman who was buried between the years 850 and 900. She most likely died in childbirth. This isn't it. This isn't what we're scared of.

Fuck you. For looking at the wrong thing, for closing the door to me.

My parents send two texts in quick succession. The first one is from my father warning about a thunderstorm over these parts and the second from my mother who wants to know if everything around these parts is okay. No one could possibly tell if they've collaborated. I reply by asking if either of them is able to estimate the rough number of people that are likely to be displaced from their homes within the next five years because of war, drought, and famine combined. 'Where?' my father says. I wait for ten minutes and stare at the relics, itching to go to the bathroom. That need comes from a different channel. I text again, telling them you've come down with a stomach bug and that they'll only be hearing you throw up if I call now. I specify that you're a very loud vomiter.

There's a smell of sweat around the Westray exhibit. They never did get to the bottom of that. Things behind glass, especially if they're old, look like all they want to do is get on with their job. What they really should do is burst, fall, decay. It is good to watch the things she left behind, to breathe, barefoot and toes wafting on cold stone, knowing that if I were Solveig, I existed. I was here and I left, but the *here* was left.

Three twenty-five am

Så här dags på natten om
jag var hon skulle jag se
till att hålla oss varma,
lyssna efter odjur och
fiender, bara överleva.

At this time of night
if I were she I would
make sure to keep us warm,
listen out for beasts and
enemies, only survive.

Jag skulle hålla armarna
mellan magen och
världen, hålla ögonen på
dig och skydda dig från
världen.

I would hold my arms
between my ---- and the
world, keep my eyes on ----
and protect ---- from the
world.

Om jag var Solveig skulle
jag lära dig, min unge,
mina favoritrefränger
redan i magen. Jag skulle
måla ett skepp på magen
och berätta en saga för
dig, om oss, efteråt.

If I were Solveig I would
teach -----, my ------, my
favourite choruses right from
the ----. I would paint a ship
on my ---- and tell ------ a
story, about us, afterward.

Four am

It wasn't just the tampon they left. The Translation Room is
a little bit like a public loo that way. If you really do desperately
have to go and there's nowhere else, you will pretend not to
notice it hasn't been flushed properly. Sit on that and then
forget. So far, I've found a tissue used on a very irritated nose,
some hairs, a copy of German *Vogue*.

You have sent three messages, each with a different version
of what basically amounts to the same question, about my
whereabouts. Instead of replying to any of them, I've been
reading this email, from a year and a half ago, which was when
you had just started the nursing course:

> In the first week of taking care of people everyone
> washes their hands all the time. In the second week,
> they cry for every lost cause, for every terminal
> diagnosis. Apparently, they say, you eventually learn to
> tell the difference between your professional self and
> yourself everywhere else, and this is how you make it.
> I think I'll try and nip that in the bud, K. This is my
> second week and I'm SO AWAKE. When that numb
> wanker comes around the corner, to take over, I'll be

ready. I'll fucking KNOW.

What is it exactly, that's safe in here?

The day Project started, you said 'Is this good?' meaning a new thing you were doing with three of the fingers on your right hand. In Swedish you would've had to say 'Does this feel good?' or it would have sounded like a religious judgement: is this GOOD? For the GOOD OF THE PEOPLE? You asked me if we could have sex lying on our sides. I remember questioning your motives, inspecting your nipples, and you said you were getting a cold and felt dizzy. You told me about someone who had webbed feet and I felt so very *with* you that I wanted to tag my forehead onto your forehead and take endless care of you. Nothing else seemed needed. Because need and knowing what someone needs do exist beyond language, and that's the part of language that bothers me the most.

Who's good at being a body anyway with all the other bodies out there? I can't be here and not with you, I can't be with you and with Project, I can't give up on the Future and carry it at the same time.

Four thirty-five am

A correction: wow, the word 'chronicle' as a verb, as in 'chronicling', does exist. There I thought I was rummaging around harmlessly. I hate it when your pal Mario talks about 'journaling'. It sounds like 'snorkelling', or 'navel-gazing'. Why doesn't he just say he keeps a journal?

190

And no more sounds from the square.

If they were here to vandalise, my torch wasn't going to stop anyone. It's not even my torch. Additionally, I've since discovered that it has no batteries, which someone else might have checked before they poked their nose out. They wouldn't find much to steal, either, as all the buildings are locked individually. Unless they blow the head off some statue, in which case: extra fun for the festival goers. They will have been so close to an exciting, dangerous night-time event.

Like the Little Mermaid in Copenhagen (which I've spent the last ten minutes reading about): the head it has now is not the head it used to have. It got sawed off in the sixties. The right arm was stolen in the eighties and then returned. Not to speak of the explosion in 2003. The question which you know is coming is, is it still the same statue? The Danish government would probably say yes. THEY would say it's still the same world.

Those people, they were very thin, wearing denim jackets. One of them even had a limp. I could call the police, but if it turns out they're just here to do a maintenance job — which they have to be, or they wouldn't have got past security — it would all get unnecessarily complicated. Joanne Tarbuck would say I was pushing it with the sucking-up. If they just wanted to see if they could, then they're already in, and I had nothing to do with it, their problem or their fun.

Four forty-seven am

Om jag var Solveig skulle   If I were Solveig I would be
jag vara på en plats,   in one place, -------- -- -
förankrad i en tid. En   ---. A necessity.
nödvöndighet.

Om jag var Solveig skulle   -- I ----- ---- I would --- be
jag vara livrädd om dig   life scared for ---

Om jag var Solveig skulle   --- -- --- ----- ---- I would
jag göra allt för dig   do anything for you

OUT THERE

Thursday

Needless to say, she missed the sun starting up and revving. First she was reading things, then she was distracted and only interested in the left-overs, then she was watching a strange film in a very cutthroat language, over and over again, till it was all one again.

Needless to say, even more than a whole desperate bunch of needless things these past few days, it was gradual. That doesn't mean it didn't happen. Once it did, it was always sudden and gradual at the same time. Yes, she thought, this is what it's like not having slept even one minute. When it got really cold, she'd rammed her fingers into her mouth, watching the film and watching the film. She'd felt her own teeth losing degrees. She was almost proud of the not-sleeping because, as she had not slept, it was still technically the same night, no turn of any page, no clean breaks, and she was still there. On the surface, nothing much had changed.

Through the really small hours, she stared at the window, trying to catch the Future as it crawled in. She did flash-runs through the nooks, raids in cupboards, but always with a glance at the window and the way the blue light adapted to each shape, rested on such different forms. She found a chocolate Bourbon, broken in five; she ate it, and then the sun was there and had obviously been there for a long time. Needless to say, there was no need for seventies Viking films anymore. The birds were so loud they could very well be sitting with their eyeballs and beaks pressed against the window, but when she opened the curtain there was nothing and no one, only an emaciated stretch of sky and some mist folding in from the sea, sexy like anything.

If this is it: she has an on-and-off relationship with the sea which can only be described in some other, ancient and useless, language.

She opened the curtains wider. Still not a single yapping bird, but on the opposite side of the square, something else came into view, spelt out in someone's best and boldest handwriting. Jesus, but it was the word *COME*. Ha. Now, because she was supposed to be a converted Christian, at least some of the time, that word could only mean salvation, grace, awesome days of joy, etc, etc. She'd be very excited and of course open the curtains all the way.

When she did, she saw a banner, attached to the Great Hall on the opposite side of the square.

WE WILL NOT BE WELL COME

it said. The rectangle of cloth was cream-coloured, the size of a small sail.

It wasn't that she didn't understand English anymore, word by word, but it did seem like it was now perched miles away, discreetly in a different part of her head. It wouldn't immediately come out of her mouth, for example, if someone stepped on her toe, or mentioned Thatcher as a feminist role model.

She went downstairs to have a look, past the hall with her old bones and accessories, and outside. She thought it was very warm, a bit grotesque, and noises came at her which couldn't mean well. Lots of seagulls, too, which were no longer sea birds these days. There was a second banner hung up across the passageway between the Scottish National War Memorial and the Royal Palace. This one was made out of someone's discarded tent.

WE WILL NOT COME WELL

This must have been when they started getting nervous last night. The letters weren't as neat as the writing on the first banner.

'Bampots,' said Hugh from maintenance.

He came along carrying a ladder and put it down for a good stare.

'A threat, most certainly,' he said.

It was too early for anyone else to be around. An alarm went off, it was about something and for someone. She wouldn't have had anything like a word for that kind of device. Solveig croaked and knew there would be an accent now. It would most likely not come well either.

'Are there … are there any more of these things?' she said.

'Aye,' Hugh said, 'Five. Covered the face of Earl Haig they did, defaced him, so to speak.'

He chuckled.

'As in, you know. You can't see his face anymore.'

'That's funny,' she said.

She pointed at the banner.

'But there's a serious problem you know,' he said.

'What?'

'You can't say anything nowadays. Can't be open about *issues*. Express your grievances.'

'A lot of people aren't well when they get here,' she said.

Shut the fick up right now, she thought. We can't be dealing with the scared bits out here and today.

There were two green threads between two of Hugh's front teeth.

'If you want to see the other ones you better hurry,' he said. 'I promise they won't last long. Give it half an hour at the most before the bosses come running. And the pregnant lasses, too.'

'The what?'

'They're angry,' he said. 'Been asked for information and it's personal.'

He picked up the ladder like it was a goat.

'Väl. Kommen. Välkommen,' Solveig said.

'Sorry, hen. Didn't realise you were on shift,' he said. 'It's the clothes.'

She wasn't wearing her own. When she turned to go back inside, she was slapped in the face by another one, right underneath the tower window. Those people in the night had managed to climb almost up to her nose.

IS IT BECAUSE WE DIDN'T INVENT FIKA?

'Who knows what it is they want,' Hugh said.

'I think maybe to be understood,' she said.

The tower looked like a swaying, swinging straw above that, awkward and implicated.

'So, you're one of them?' said Hugh. 'I thought you worked in there, in the office.'

'My Translation Room is up there,' she said.

'Decent view,' said Hugh.

'I have to keep the curtains drawn.'

'I see you come in early. The others don't come in so early. Are you an addict?'

'I'm a Norse person,' she said.

He grinned. Yes, thank god, that *was* the right reaction.

'Well you don't look like one,' he said.

'That's kind of you to say,' she said.

'Lord knows how they decide who they hire,' he said.

If this is Solveig: everything she needs is on this rock. The whole itinerary of work and living and defending is between these fortified walls and nothing horrifying is going to sneak into that. She will do the milking first. That's it, dealt with.

It wasn't fun admitting to, but sometimes, in the *before,* she'd been repelled by the slow-streaming, hot smell of the cows. *Now* was nothing like that. On this side of last night, the cows' breaths were smooth, hot on her belly, and she knew what each sound meant. Every turn of their heads was something they'd heard, smelt, or just knew, and it was her job to check it to keep them safe. That film she'd watched before, the hideous one with the majestic hairs, made it seem like milk coming straight out of a cow is tempting and delicious. There's a short sequence in which film-Solveig gulps it down from the bowl, but in real life the milk is too internal for most people. Before, she had never thought about this. Now, when she put her tongue inside the bowl and flicked it, it made her want to cry, how this wasn't for her, how the milk went missing because the calf was gone.

'Where do we even start?' she said to them. 'Where do we even ficking begin?'

Ingrid and Algot came in at the same time, both free of headgear. It struck Solveig that Algot was always going to lose his good back at a young age.

'Have you seen them?' said Algot. 'It's the Lithuanians, isn't it, isn't it?'

Ingrid kept mumbling things and stamping the dirt in the wrong part of the house. Her hands were very wrinkly.

'They'll get us all fired,' said Algot. 'It's really not a joke.'

'Good morning,' Solveig said. 'I'm not laughing.'

Algot stretched both hands to the house gods in the ceiling.

'But what do you *think* about it?' Solveig said and handed him a mug of milk.

He retched and pushed the mug away so that some of it was spilt on her clothes.

'I'm so sorry about that,' Solveig said to the cows.

'What is this?' he said.

She looked over at Ingrid who was peering out through the byre door.

'They've opened the gates, too,' Algot said. 'The idiots. If people are allowed in, they'll always, always come in.'

The first few days of the festivals are rammed every year. Three guides with yellow umbrellas, each holding a cardboard cut-out of a pointing finger, had already marched past at the head of their hoards. One of them, Solveig was sure, was wearing sunglasses on top of regular glasses. She clearly couldn't see where she was going. A Canadian group turned straight in to begin their tour in the byre, immediately filling up the whole hut. A woman with rucksacks both front and back seemed to take offence at the lack of space. A fake skinned rabbit got stolen from the dwelling-house, too, the fifth one in as many years to go missing.

'This is a horrid environment,' Algot said and fought his way out.

'That's something else for us to think about,' she said to the cows. 'We don't know what that word means do we?'

She went after him. People didn't make particular room for her. Outside, it seemed that something had come and stripped the place naked at high speed, a quiet desert storm.

'Where are they?' Algot said, walking toward Argyle Battery.

'Who?' said Ingrid.

It was a little bit easier to understand her today. Could be that the change stretched to Icelandic?

'The staff,' said Algot.

There were plenty of tourists milling around but no sign of People. Every French, Polish, and Irish seemed to have

201

dissipated between mobile phones and camera lenses.

'I'm going to ask someone,' Solveig was almost a hundred percent sure Ingrid said.

Ingrid went off carrying her staff horizontally between two families.

'What's wrong with you?' Algot said. 'You sound like you have a cold.'

But what do we say? That it *feels* different?

They found the rest of the staff on Argyle Battery, at least twenty or so of them so far, addressing each other, asking, listening, and finding out in gushing English, with absolutely no shame sticking to any of their dancing lips. There was so much blabbering that it went all the way inside the ear straight away and started splashing, past all border controls.

'They're everywhere!' Ingrid hissed. 'There are more by the cannons.'

She meant the banners. As a side: no, it wasn't any easier to understand Icelandic today after all. Unfortunately, Ingrid had just been speaking English this whole time.

'Oh, mother-in-law,' said Solveig in an attempt to bring everything back.

'What?' said Ingrid. 'Did you know about this?'

WE ARE HERE

one of the banners said.

Ingrid sat down on a piece of wall and took a shoe off. She was distracting herself. People do that, Solveig thought, when things become way too truthful, they distract and distract themselves.

'They've started recruiting among the cleaners,' she said.

'For what?' Solveig said.

Ingrid held the shoe up to Solveig's face. She didn't want to see Solveig's face when she said this.

'Mothers,' Ingrid said.

She gestured with the shoe toward Solveig's belly.

Om detta är hon skulle hon bry sig om vad som händer där ute?	If this is she, would she care about what goes on out there?

Word had it that someone was seen during the night, caught by a particular CCTV camera which was supposed to be out of order. Anyway, nobody was meant to know which cameras worked or were out of order. Most people suspected the Lithuanians, regardless.

'Have you heard the giggles?' Algot said.

They were all speaking English now, had been doing for a while, and nobody had exploded. They did sound beside themselves, though, set to one side like salads.

'Or the Polish,' said Algot. 'It could definitely be the Polish because they have this history.'

His neck was all sunburnt, it looked hot to the touch.

'Are you saying you like it here?' Solveig said. 'Are you saying you like the way things work?'

'I still think the Italians,' said Algot. 'That would be my guess.'

'Or management, perhaps?' Ingrid said. 'I wouldn't. What do you say?'

'Put it past them,' said Solveig. 'I wouldn't put it past them.'

'A lovely expression,' Ingrid said.

In English she gesticulated, as if she was having to constantly hail taxis.

It smelt like lavender in the dwelling-house now. Just while they'd been out someone had brought that in. Algot went straight over to check on his gear and found that the sword was missing.

'Fucking fuck,' he said.

'Oh baby,' Ingrid said.

There was a boy-shadow in the doorway. If Niklas ever has to visit the Castle when he's not on shift, he never comes inside the house, in part because the normal clothes seem to infuriate the chicken.

'My god, this day, guys,' he said. 'Have you heard about the Lithuanians?'

He'd come for his P46. He'd been offered a temporary role in a play and he was past taking the safe road, he said, then he took a little bow.

'What's with Joanne Tarbuck, by the way? I said hello and I thought she was going to slap me.'

This was when he looked over at Solveig and saw the belly, a less-than-a-week-old miracle which Solveig's body temperature had finally adjusted to. She had taken to cradling it and cradling her backache, which was its own bundle, all at once.

'Nice,' he said. 'Hilarious. You know I really believed you, when you told me about that research thing you were doing?'

'What research thing?' said Algot. 'Are you doing an Ingrid?'

'She told me she was pregnant. Then she told me she was finding out about maternity leave policies in corporations.'

'I *am* pregnant,' Solveig said.

'What's your problem?' said Algot.

He found his sword in a rubbish bin, hugged it tight, and left without saying anything else. Nobody asked him what he meant to do with the sword at a time like this. Ingrid pinched the skin between her eyes and began rearranging the steatite bowls.

'Are you sure you're not going to die?' Solveig said.

'Fifteen bloody years in this place,' Ingrid said.

A Japanese group streamed inside and began rummaging through the sacks of grain. Sometimes group guides arrange treasure hunts and then forget where they buried the prizes. Once, Solveig found a pack of desiccated chocolate coins and a ticket to the Camera Obscura in one of those sacks.

'You know how I feel about atmosphere,' someone said walking past.

'I know, I know, I'm sorry,' someone replied.

When Algot came back from the loo, he offered a short report of the situation with the banners. Some of them could be seen from the middle of Princes Street, including one that said *THIS IS YOUR PROBLEM* which really wasn't good news. People were gathering down there.

'What is this then,' Niklas said pointing at the belly. 'A pay rise?'

There was bird crap on his shoulder. She could tell the exact moment when two or three people standing around the

205

dwelling-house noticed this, and not one of them pointed it out to him.

'I *am* sorry,' she said. 'But you didn't have to get involved. You could have just translated what I said to her.'

'Whatever you say,' he said. 'Say hi to Ciaran from me.'

You've met, what, never? Arsehorse.

'Do you want to know how it feels?' she said and took his hand to place it on the belly.

He pulled it back and looked at her, but not quite at her, like she only deserved those kinds of smiles from now on, for ever and ever.

A few minutes later, two members of the management team turned up, wanting a word. They asked the tourists to wait outside for just a moment. They had lattes for themselves and tote bags which they handed over to the tourists as recompense for the inconvenience. Then they stood still and tightly together, right in the middle of the dwelling-house.

'The walls are perfectly clean,' Ingrid said.

'I think,' one of them said, looking at the last skinned rabbit, 'that we can all agree none of this is good for business.'

'Which means it's good for no one,' said the other.

'We're of course not saying you did it,' said the first.

Ingrid was smiling.

'Gary,' she said gently. 'How's your wee girl these days? She fell off her horse, didn't she?'

Gary flinched and put both his hands in his pockets.

'Inger?' he said glancing at a notebook the other one was

holding. 'That's your name I believe?'

Solveig was standing right next to Ingrid. She couldn't get over the buoyancy of Ingrid's voice like this, today, so light, and how far out it reached. She wondered in which language Ingrid had been sick and recovered. She decided to ask her soon, because she could now. She held her fingers pressed into the small of her back, where a little pain was beginning to amass. The pain took a deep breath and then a large bite out of her.

She had seen him once, that Gary man, knitting socks at a bus stop in Fountainbridge. He had a way of biting down on his Ss which made him sound like he was thirsty. The other guy said 'so' at the beginning of practically everything. Together they were a really sheet chorus.

'We only just got here,' Algot said.

'We know you all talk to each other,' the other guy said. 'But today that's not the problem.'

'What have you heard?' said Gary.

'It's a protest,' Solveig said. 'I didn't hear that. Nobody told me that.'

'Please don't take it personally,' Gary said. 'Look Simon here is from China.'

'I've just joined you as HR manager,' Simon said.

Solveig took a little step and then another little step, almost all the way up to him. The pain, again, started chewing on her pelvic floor with its molars.

'Fick!' she said.

'Excuse me?' he said.

'Us?' she said. 'You're joining *us*?'

'Well, not you specifically,' Simon said and looked terrified.

'Stop!' Solveig said, right into the man's face.

Something was seeping through and out. Something undecided and uncertain, not quite liquid, was leaking. She suspected that her eyes were very wide by now and she took a step back from the man.

'Shit,' she said.

Out of her came a tickling little membrane, not anything as full-on as a flood, but more of a soap-bubble bursting. Very soon, she was holding herself up only by clenching every single muscle bellow her belly button, including her fists, making the pain worse, but it didn't make any difference. She thought of hourglasses, it kept dripping so slowly and non-stop.

'Shit, not now,' she said again.

'We wouldn't want to single anyone out,' said Gary. 'But this affects everyone negatively, including you. We're all in this together.'

She looked over at Ingrid and Ingrid, god damn her, took Solveig's hand.

'Is there anything that you need?' she said, her fingers around the fleshiest bit of Solveig's upper arm. It felt like she was being carefully dressed.

'What's wrong with you?' Gary said.

'I need, maybe, a hospital,' Solveig said.

'Just give us five minutes.'

'Are you joking?' Ingrid said.

'I think it's safe to say it can wait five minutes, yes?'

208

'How on earth do you know what's safe?' Solveig said.

Ingrid ushered her out. She didn't ask, just pushed along with two fingers firmly between Solveig's shoulder blades. The day was hotter now.

om jag var Solveig skulle jag veta vad jag borde göra	if I were Solveig I'd know what to do
om jag var Solveig skulle jag veta vem jag borde rädda	if I were Solveig I'd know who to save

Fick it, why does it take so much longer to say that in Swedish?

Lady Gaga and Björn Skifs let themselves out. She only opened the door. As they were walking past her, she spotted an ugly-looking sore, then a limp, then a scratched area, all red and blistered. She was worried about making it worse so she didn't touch any of it. They had all been doing nothing but their jobs and then these things had happened, all this non-understanding layered on top. The cows pressed her against the door as they walked out, uninterested in her excuses, but possibly smelling the blood.

att höra hemma   to belong

att höra hemma   to hear at home

So, what does that say about listening?

She thought she'd get on a bus, with the layers hopefully barricading the blood flow for another half hour or so. It wasn't even halfway pouring and to be honest, she felt fine. It was more like a resolute shifting and still under control, enough to maybe leave a stain on the seat but not enough for anyone to notice it until after she'd got off.

'Something happened here,' they would think. 'Nothing has been done about it. What a disgrace for Lothian Bus Services.'

She followed the main trail of people toward the exit. A girl started squawking, a bit like Ingrid's made-up yodelling but more, well, southern was the word that came up. She'd go to the hospital and put herself in the hands of clean, white-robed competence. Golly, she couldn't wait for the white robes and especially the solid competence. She pictured it as having very lean muscles and, surprisingly, humming along to 'Girls Just Want To Have Fun'. They would put their hands on her when necessary and it would all just be another part of their day. They would find her case, this event, so very normal, almost boring. They would be thinking about their dinners and they'd fix things in no time. This was the plan — to be under control. She didn't think of any of the robes as yours; she didn't have someone like you in mind.

Now Barbara, Barbara with her uniform all covered in streaks of paint, ran into her as she was passing the cannons. Those things didn't look large enough for anyone to hide behind anymore.

'Coming or going?' Barbara said, as if Solveig had been the one legging it.

One of Barbara's cheeks was flushed, but no way was it because of a fist. In this place hitting surely had never happened. Solveig had always wondered about Barbara's high heels — why, and how often, and weren't they really unnecessary? That was the kind of thing you thought on a regular Thursday.

'You're barefoot,' Solveig said.

'See you down there,' Barbara said.

'Woah, woah, woah,' Solveig said, as the blood started coming down faster and there was more of it. Barbara was on her way, she said, to fetch some old uniforms from the stock room, anything they could hang up and write on. There wasn't going to be anything left next week for the burning of another Einar. Nothing at all for the fickers to use as props in their theatres.

> If I were you, would I be
> coming or going?

That's not a thing people say in Swedish.

The path down to the Portcullis Gate was bottlenecked, mostly with French aristocrats, two of whom were ripping off their corsets, and about ten box-office assistants. Together, they

212

could make you think the world, these days, was divided into wars and brothels, and that you'd missed that happening as well. A minute later, they weren't even that separate. Solveig thought she saw an Irish dock worker wearing a box-office suit jacket, with nothing else underneath but a raging, red scar, the texture of corals. Then one of the box-office assistants was riding piggy-back on that Spanish girl who shared Solveig's Translation Room. She was wearing a belly, too. They ran like that all the way down to the gate, where about forty people sat, half of them cleaners. At least ten of them wore bellies on top of their uniforms. Above them, four new signs had appeared:

YOU ARE HOME   *ESTAS EN TU CASA*
আপনবাড়ীতে   *TAI JŪSŲ NAMAI*

they said.

Solveig thought they looked like eyes pried open, each holding a worst nightmare and its way out. It would have looked more professional without the present-wrapping string holding them up. She stopped next to a guy who was filming it. He was talking to himself, without pausing for breath. English was careening out of him in between his clenched teeth. One of the cleaners, a large man with his fake belly hanging halfway down his side, stood up and began to shout things he had no idea how to pronounce. He was hollering it like an auctioneer. Two management people ran past Solveig, both with their phones plastered to their ears. They were followed by three security guards.

'If you look closely,' this tiny woman said nearby, 'they're not really that fit are they?'

The guards went for the sign written in English first.

They aimed straight at the word *HOME* with a rubber hose. Its dusty body must not have seen the light of day in a decade, it was cracked and spilt at the mouth, but it did the job. One of the guards had a broomstick which she used to hammer and scratch at the words until the paint began to disintegrate. At first, there were only a couple of scattered 'no!'s and 'please!'s, the rest of it a plastered silence, keeping all their throats in line.

Solveig thought: I should really be getting away now.

Solveig thought: but I can't.

Barbara was there now; she sat down right in front of the Lithuanian sign, her nose a water hydrant, and Daryl Urban, whose name was never Daryl Urban. He walked up to the guard who was swinging the broomstick and was shoved aside by another one coming from behind. He was wearing flip-flops underneath all that culture, orange ones, which made him slip. When he got back up, he stepped close to the guard and said something quietly. He made sure they knew his hands were asleep in front of him and would never move.

om jag hör hemma här   if I belong here

The security guard said 'Stand back!' in Daryl Urban's face, then she took a little nervous step sideways, a toe-to-toe shuffle which hardly anyone saw but she clearly knew she had done. The other two security guards came up and grabbed Daryl Urban from behind. Solveig reached for her phone, thinking there might be some battery left and knowing it was very unlikely. She'd made a point of not charging it so that she couldn't check for messages through the night.

'Sir, step back now!'

'We live here!'

The phone was dead, as expected.

The signs had all been tied to unused hooks on the structure of the walls, small crevices and shapes of metal which at some point in this place's history must have had a purpose, probably to do with defence. One of the strings, holding the corner of the Bengali sign, came off in the wind and the whole thing folded over like an exhausted eyelid. The back of the fabric was stained orange and green. Looking closer, they were definitely a child's drawing of a dinosaur.

'No pictures!' Joanne Tarbuck howled.

If I were Solveig: I'd be running for my safety now.

If I were Solveig: I'd be running for our safety now.

Solveig waved at Joanne Tarbuck as she raced past. She had two more security guards with her. Solveig pretended she was taking a picture of that, of her, with her dead phone and that's when Joanne Tarbuck started walking toward her, mouth shut, all elbows and a security guard in tow. Solveig backed up toward the Bengali banner. A shield of people was already forming around it, with a couple of them, in cleaning uniforms, trying to re-attach the sign. She turned, belly out, in front of those people, to protect those people. She was standing with all these quiet, pissed-off people, maybe afraid, maybe surprised by the way their arms found themselves hooked around the arm of other people they didn't like very much, maybe extremely put off by the sweaty crooks of the arms of those people,

and I saw you, squeezed into this.   och jag såg dig, inkämd i detta.

You were helping reattach the Spanish sign which was flapping, too, picked up by the wind and spanked about in your face. Even so, your face was unlocked, stunned halfway between a smile and a what-the-fuck-is-this, now, K? You'd somehow managed to shave half your head really badly.

Joanne Tarbuck kept trying to reach the sign to yank it down.

'Sorry?' I heard you say. 'Pardon me?'

You and Joanne Tarbuck continued your awkward tug of war for way too long. It was ficking excruciating. And while that happened I watched you, not as you are with me in our hideously minute world, but very briefly as you are out there, to someone who doesn't know you, who knows nothing about you, who neither has nor thinks they need any words for what you are, but maybe needs something from you. Your body was a colour which makes some people ask where you're from and others wonder what you're doing here, your hands pretty square, a tattoo behind your left ear, suspicious with the what and the who and the where. Everything everyone else has made you was there, chucked in with the misunderstandings, the wrong words and the almost-right ones.

'Seriously,' I said to Ingrid who'd just shown up next to me (and by the way, I was happy to see her, but where had *she* been all this time?), 'he's clearly only trying to help.'

'Weren't you going to a hospital?' Ingrid said then.

It was dizzying, and so much like an arrival, that I just stood there for a while, with one hand on the belly and the other on this guy's naked shoulder, which was bobbing up and down as all of him shook.

'Behöver du hjälp?'   'Do you need help?'

I heard you say to Joanne Tarbuck.

You thought maybe *that* would get through to her? Joanne Tarbuck looked like she was about to throw up on your hand. I couldn't hear her very well, almost not at all, in fact, but I think she said something like 'huh?' or 'what?' or 'excuse me?'

OUT DÄR

We are home now. It's late again and early tomorrow. Is this what it will be like for you with night shifts? Truthfully, I never thought about the night shifts till now. Arsehorse.

When we got to the hospital, I walked in belly first. You'd asked if I was going to take it off on the bus and I said, 'No thank you'. It could be useful against the road bumps and sudden halts. Those also seemed to make the blood do something differently. It felt rushed. You suggested we take a taxi and I said I was still strongly in favour of a bus. You said okay, but that we had to sit in the middle where the ups and downs were less noticeable. I said that was boats you were thinking of and you proceeded to tell me about when you were in Shetland and learnt about a group of puffins who never knew what was best for them.

'I used one of those once,' you said and nodded toward the belly. 'At a Halloween party when I was playing Evil Santa.'

'This one cost £300,' I said, 'It didn't come from Amazon.'

I felt it was fair to Joanne Tarbuck to communicate that to you.

'The clothes are cool,' you said. 'It's been a long time since I've seen the clothes. I like these bits.'

You poked carefully at the brooches. I took one off and put it in your hand to show you how much lighter it is than it looks.

They've done such a great job with it.

The guy at reception had super-crafted nails, with tiny shapes of Christmas trees on them, even though it's August. His upper lip sparkled. He typed me into some system and made us both feel very welcome.

'It wouldn't surprise me at all if he used to work in hospitality,' I said. 'Casinos.'

'There's a stain,' you said and looked at the back of my pinafore.

Once I'd explained about what was happening, everything moved quickly. They took me away; they did an ultrasound. By 'they' I mean this one, small woman, but she had the anonymous touch of so many different people, maybe because of the gloves.

'How did you two meet, then?' she asked.

You said I'd found you on my gap-year travels.

'Oh no,' I said. 'Ciaran.'

'In a home for addicts in Delhi,' you said.

She disliked you instantly, for all the wrong reasons.

She said Project was, is, still ongoing, and there is still a choice we could make. For a while, they left us waiting in a consultation room, just the two of us, you swinging your legs off the side of the stretcher, talking about how, just after I'd left last night, a bus had broken down right outside the window and there had been a voice coming out of it:

'This bus is under attack,' the voice had said.

'Who the fuck would phrase it *that* way?' you said. 'It would just make things so much worse.'

'That's not what you're supposed to say,' I said. 'Not you.'

I was massaging my back against a door handle. I saw the print of a thumb on it, only to realise seconds later that it could only be yours or mine.

If we were only slightly different, if we hadn't made each other the way we are, I would spend hours and hours wondering what they would look like, our kid. What colour the bit of bony surface behind their ears would be, where so much crap gathers. How much would they object to being hugged in semi-public spaces? Would they wonder how coal mines were ever a thing people knew about without crying? Would they develop an allergy to your favourite early-2000s gangster rap, and would they tell me if they did?

'Hospitals are like that, too,' I said.

'Like what?' you said.

'Places you go and never come back from,' I said.

You walked across to the other side of the room, where the sink was, got up on the tips of your toes, and then walked back again. You disinfected your hands once more.

'Hey,' you said, 'have you noticed how there's like a set number of ways people deal with waiting in hospitals? There's the nervous type, the one that carries around the cups of tea for everyone. There's the people who cry, I mean *only* cry. The one on the phone with a pal, talking about video games or something, because he doesn't want to think about what's going on inside that room.'

'You've missed work today,' I said.

'Yes,' you said. 'I've made arrangements.'

'You can't,' I said. 'You can't do that for everything.'

'Kristin,' you said. 'Are we not really fucking trying?'

This one nurse backed into the room with a wee cart and didn't notice we were in there until she'd almost backed into me.

I thought: if I were Solveig the bump would have put a stop to that in no time.

When she'd left, full of excuses, I said to you:

'This is the first time I've ever been to a hospital, for myself I mean. I never broke any bones.'

'You should have gone straight to the hospital.'

'Actually, no,' I said. 'I should have stayed longer. They were taking people away.'

'All the other people weren't already bleeding,' you said.

'Someone grabbed Daryl Urban,' I said.

'Who's Daryl Urban?'

'A guy I work with.'

'What if you'd lost it?' you said.

'I thought about that,' I said. 'Even before I saw you.'

höra hemma   hear home/ here home

I went over to you, studying the plasticity of the floor and not your face yet. I sat down next to you and we swung our legs in tandem. One, two, three, four. One, two, three. The doctor was taking ages and your stomach began to rumble. I was still reeling from the technical bone term you'd used out in the waiting room. It sounded like people might believe you when you told them what was likely to be wrong with them.

'You know,' you said, 'I just thought of something else.'

'Go on,' I said.

'Living with you is like being a kid and getting to play with your best friend every day, but as an adult.'

'Yes!' I said. 'That, exactly that.'

'Do you think that if our kid wanted to learn Portuguese, that it would be easier for them because of my genes?' you said. 'I never tried.'

'Hm,' I said.

You breathed in. I stayed as I was. You didn't exhale for a while, not until you got it.

'Not this kid,' you said. 'Not ours. Not the way things are now.'

'No,' I said.

'When did you decide?'

'I'm still,' I said.

'Am I,' you said, 'am I an arse for asking if you're sure?'

'Nope.'

I must have looked like a racoon again, because you said:

'We *will* still be here,' and then you put your face in your hands, strange shoreline across your head fully exposed. You must have accidentally changed the guard on the clippers halfway through.

'Did you finish with the slug?' I said.

The nurse came in, the right one this time, tired face first. I made an appointment for Monday.

'That was funny,' I said. 'It was so funny, when you tried to speak Swedish to Joanne Tarbuck.'

'Well she wouldn't fuckin' explain,' you said, 'she just kept yelling. I tried French, too. I don't know how things work in that place.'

'I forgot to tell you but I think Mrs Pullingham is her mother.'

'Fantastic!' you said and refused to move. 'I wonder if they're like each other?'

'But it was so funny,' I said, 'when you spoke Swedish to her.'

You took a whole wad of brochures with you on our way out and tucked them into every one of your pockets, including one about incontinence and one about spinal injuries.

OUT THERE

Denise singing 'Twa Corbies' at one am and not giving a flying fick.

The foul-mouthed foxes on our street having a rally.

The wombats in Australia allowing other animals to use their burrows during a crisis.

The orphanage in São Paulo where you were small.

One billion refugees.

Ingrid's silicone breasts.

My parent's financial panic.

The Future.

You

IN HERE

Denise singing 'Twa Corbies' at one in the morning and not giving a flying fick.

The foul-mouthed foxes on our street having a rally.

The wombats in Australia allowing other animals to use their burrows.

The orphanage where you began.

One billion climate refugees.

Ingrid's silicone breasts.

My parent's financial panic.

The Future.

You.

Between five and six o'clock this morning, in the Translation Room, I deleted every single one of your old emails. It was really stupid and I regret it now, so much that I might never tell you about it.

It's after one am and everything below the level of my clavicles can't wait to tune out, just be ficking switched off and turned down for a long time. Even the idea of falling asleep, after twenty-four hours of not sleeping, looks like a door you're about to go through, with who knows what behind it except not more of the same, never more of the same.

There's definitely something odd going on with Denise. I'm convinced she's standing right below the window, midnight-drunk and howling the same two lines over and over again about the 'Bonnie blue een' and the hair. For what? In the hope that someone will notice and open their window to shout, 'Hey pal, it's the wrong bloody song'? How can we possibly sleep through that? How can we not go out to make sure she's all right?

Don't think I haven't noticed that we've already started to use words we didn't, one at a time, something thrown over the shoulder. An idiotic phrase comes out of you and I don't leap to stop it quite as fanatically as before. You make a Swedish word sound almost like you, but not quite, never quite the same, obviously, and sometimes you do other things:

'Att somna,' you said, 'to fall asleep but without the falling or the going to sleep? Just, what, sleepifying? That's very efficient of you people.'

'To asleep,' I said.

'To asleepen,' you said.

I go check on Denise. I come back having lost her to the rest of it. Who knows how we'll be in the morning, except not the same, obviously, never quite the same again.

Gratitude

has a soft reputation, as found among incense sticks in esoteric shops. My gratitude to those who built this book, directly or indirectly, is the most solid thing. You are behind every bit that's good. Thank you

to everyone at Scribe, especially my editor Molly Slight for a winning combination of listening and confidence. To my agent, Lisa Baker, for your intuition, beautiful honesty and battle cries. To Philip Gwyn Jones for reading and believing, and to Allison Colpoys for dressing the story in your art. To early pals of the wee beasty: Kim Sherwood, Nicholas Herrmann, and Naomi Ishiguro. To Andrew Jones and Hannah Sackett for guidance when researching Norse life in Scotland. To Shabana Khanam, Unnur Ósk Kristinsdóttir, and Rūta Nanartavičiūtė for much appreciated assistance with translations to Bengali, Icelandic, and Lithuanian in the book. To my colleagues at Mr B's over the last few years, in particular Henry Tottle for transporting the desk used, to Emma Smith for the unquestionable prescience of your arm-hairs, to Ed Scotland for the word 'crenulations' and many other stories, and to Tom Mooney for your joyous enthusiasm (please don't throw this book across the room).

Tack till Ylva Marsh för så många lugn. Tack, Elix 'Emi min' Hwang, livssyskon och medresenär.

Muchas gracias a mi familia en Colombia, por risas y apoyo desde lejos och till farmor och farfar för stöd sedan länge. Tack, Jennifer Johannesson, systra min, för att du finns. Tack till mina föräldrar, Olga och Rolf Johannesson, for showing me the joy and the love in crossing borders.

Thank you to my Person, Adam Ley-Lange, who didn't ask me where I *really* came from, but what I cared about. For every single day.